BACCA AND THE RIDDLE OF THE DIAMOND DRAGON

AN UNOFFICIAL NOVEL

BACCA
AND THE RIDDLE OF THE DIAMOND DRAGON

AN UNOFFICIAL MINECRAFTER'S ADVENTURE

JEROMEASF

SKY PONY PRESS
NEW YORK

Sky Pony Press books may be purchased in bulk at special discounts for sales promotion, corporate gifts, fund-raising, or educational purposes. Special editions can also be created to specifications. For details, contact the Special Sales Department, Sky Pony Press, 307 West 36th Street, 11th Floor, New York, NY 10018 or info@ skyhorsepublishing.com.

Sky Pony® is a registered trademark of Skyhorse Publishing, Inc.®, a Delaware corporation.

Visit our website at www.skyponypress.com.

10 9 8 7 6 5 4 3 2 1

Library of Congress Cataloging-in-Publication Data is available on file.

Cover design by Brian Peterson

Cover artwork by Josh Bruce (www.inkbyte.net)

Print ISBN: 978-1-5107-0398-8

Ebook ISBN: 978-1-5107-0399-5

Printed in Canada

chapter one

The zombie took a step forward.

Bacca smiled and waited. So did the crowd of spectators sitting in the amphitheater around him.

The zombie took another step across the raised platform. Then another. Then another still.

In his hand, Bacca held his most prized possession in the entire Overworld—a glistening diamond axe named "Betty." It shimmered in the light of the moon above, and felt perfectly balanced in Bacca's hands . . . almost like it was a part of him. Betty had seen Bacca through many adventures, and proved itself worthy of every challenge. If a finer weapon existed anywhere, Bacca did not know of it.

Bacca carefully took aim at the zombie. The watching crowd could no longer contain their excitement.

"What's he going to do to the zombie?" someone asked expectantly. "Can you see?"

"I wonder what he's waiting for?" asked another.

"Is that *Betty*?" asked a third. "Ooh, it's all . . . sparkly, like!"

The crowd didn't know exactly what they were there to see, but that was part of the appeal. With

Bacca in charge, they knew that, whatever it was, it was going to be something good.

In addition to being talented with an axe, Bacca was the most celebrated crafter in the entire Minecraft universe. He was always constructing staggering, inventive environments that bordered on the unbelievable. Glistening skyscrapers. Endless labyrinths. Treetop canopies that seemed to extend forever into the sky. And Bacca always built these things with his friends in mind. People from servers all over the Overworld came to marvel at his creations. He also had a devilish sense of fun. Some of his creations were pranks or tricks. You never knew precisely what you were going to get with Bacca. That was part of what made him such a showman.

The zombie on the platform took another drunken, staggering step toward Bacca. Betty gleamed brightly in the moonlight. And then descended.

Striking at precisely the right moment, Bacca skillfully knocked the zombie off the side of the platform, down a chute he had created out of blocks of wooden planks. The zombie tumbled back and forth comically along the chute until it was spat out into an alley . . . leading to a triangle of carefully crafted iron pins. The zombie collided against them and made a satisfying sound. The iron pins toppled over. The crowd began to cheer.

"Zombie bowling!" said someone. "Well, that's a new one. I like it!"

"I *wondered* what those pins were for," said another. "In retrospect, I suppose it should have been obvious."

"Looks like he bowled a strike to me," said a third.

Bacca gazed on in satisfaction as the crowd around him expressed their pleasure in his latest Minecraft construction. Coming up with new ways to be creative never got old for him. The possibilities of Minecraft seemed endless. It was merely up to Bacca to discover them.

Later, after the crowd had left, Bacca strode alone through the empty amphitheater with his girlfriend, LadyBacc, and wondered what his next creation might be. How would he top himself? What would he do next?

"Zombie bowling was a hit," said LadyBacc enthusiastically. "I totally knew it would be."

"I guess," said Bacca sheepishly. "I always feel pressure to do better. I don't want to let the audience down. Know what I mean?"

"Do better?" she replied skeptically. "For a guy who looks like a hairy bear wearing a three piece suit, I think you've done very well for yourself."

"You're just saying that because you look like a hairy bear in a dress," he pointed out.

"I'm being serious," said LadyBacc. "Think about it. You've got millions of fans who come to watch the things that you create. You're one of the most famous crafters in all of Minecraft—maybe the *most* famous."

"Yeah," said Bacca. "I suppose so. It's just important to me that I give people a good show."

"I think you worry too much," LadyBacc said with a laugh. "Everything you build always ends up being awesome. I'm sure you'll come up with something great for your next crafting project. You always do."

"I guess you're right," Bacca said. "Thanks for the encouragement."

"No problem!"

They agreed to meet up later in the week, but for the moment, Bacca was tired from all the day's exciting events, and decided to retire for the evening.

To his castle.

Perched on the edge of a cliff overlooking a beautiful placid sea, the castle had ten towers reaching gloriously into the skies above. On top of the highest tower was a spire, and on the spire was a flag with a giant "B." The three moats surrounding the castle contained flowing lava, water, and then lava again for good measure. Bacca easily bounded over them as he traced the familiar path back to his front door. (Any zombies or skeletons that came his way would not be so lucky.)

Hopping through his front hallway, he first made for the castle's kitchen.

Bacca's kitchen was unlike typical ones, in that it generally resembled a large aquarium. As the familiar blue glow came into view, Bacca's stomach started growling. He took a moment to enjoy the appetizing sight of the salmon, clownfish, and pufferfish that all bobbed in front of him in the enormous glass tank.

It would be an understatement to say that Bacca's favorite food was raw fish. It was more like his *only* food. Bacca had a hard time understanding why somebody would eat anything else. Maybe the appeal of raw fish had something to do with Bacca's hairy, animal-like appearance. Maybe it was because it was the closest thing you could get to sushi in Minecraft. Or maybe it was just because it tasted totally delicious.

Bacca took out his favorite fishing pole from a rack on the wall and dangled his line into the enormous tank. His rod was enchanted with Lure, Luck of the Sea, and Unbreaking. Probably *this* was why the fish came right to him . . . but Bacca liked to think that it was also because of his excellent fishing skills.

When he had made a good-sized pile of fish beside him, Bacca put away the rod and began to dig in. Bacca ate with his hands, enjoying the feel of the slippery fish in his claws and relishing ripping each one open with his teeth. So delicious! Again, he wondered why anybody would eat anything else!

After finishing the final fish, Bacca burped loudly, and headed up to his bedroom for some well-earned rest. On the way, he passed through the castle hallways overflowing with chests full of souvenirs from his many adventures. Some he had crafted himself, and others he had found, but each piece was designed to remind him of one of his awesome escapades throughout the Overworld.

Bacca climbed a sandstone staircase to the highest tower in his castle and finally arrived in the bedroom. He had a four-poster bed decorated with dark prismarine and gold. Bacca couldn't wait to jump in. Bed was the place that his best crafting ideas usually came to him. What new creation would he dream up for tomorrow? Bacca was excited to find out!

Bacca took a running start and prepared to bound into bed . . . but a strange, sudden sound made him hesitate. It was a flapping, like giant wings cutting through the atmosphere. The noise was distant, but getting louder with each moment.

There was a single window set into the wall of Bacca's bedroom. He hurried over and took a look at the landscape outside. Something very large rushed past the window. It was enormous, shiny, and moving very fast.

"What in the Overworld was that?" Bacca wondered out loud. But inside he already knew.

Dragon!

Being a master crafter, Bacca was no stranger to dragons. In fact, one of Bacca's favorite games to play was "Dragon Escape" in which he and his friends lured an Ender Dragon into a biome they had created. Then they tried to evade it as it chased them around a complicated parkour course. It was great fun!

But dragons almost never showed up unannounced like this. What was this one doing here, at Bacca's castle, in the middle of the night?

The dragon made another circle around Bacca's bedroom tower. Bacca watched it go by. Just to make sure, he looked for the telltale wings, long tail, and giant teeth. Yep. There they were. *Definitely* a dragon.

But something was strange in the way its bright, crystal skin caught the light. Almost like it was . . . like it was . . .

Bacca did not have time to complete the thought.

Without warning, the dragon began to descend through the top of Bacca's bedroom! The stone bricks it touched either exploded or melted away. The dragon knew what it was doing, digging down to find Bacca's position. When Bacca's roof was completely destroyed, the dragon hovered above him in midair.

The best way to kill a dragon was with a bow and arrows, but Bacca was an axe-guy. Besides, his bow was in a chest somewhere downstairs. Bacca considered his options. It would be easy to head down the winding staircase and outrun the dragon, but then it might follow him—and wreck his awesome castle that he'd so painstakingly crafted.

Before Bacca could arrive at a firm decision, the enormous dragon did something he'd never seen a dragon do before. It spoke.

"Hello," it said in a voice as deep as an ocean trench. "Are you Bacca?"

Bacca was surprised, but only for a second.

"What's this about?" Bacca replied coolly. "You just smashed up my roof. You got blocks everywhere. And what if it rains tonight? Seriously. Not cool."

"Sorry," the dragon said sheepishly. "I wouldn't normally do something like this."

"That's *exactly* what you would normally do," Bacca replied skeptically. "You're a *dragon*."

"I guess so," the dragon said. "But I'm only here because it's an emergency."

"Oh yeah?" said Bacca. "What *kind* of emergency?"

The dragon hesitated.

"Also," Bacca added, "am I crazy, or are you *made of diamonds*?"

"Yes," the dragon said. "I am."

It was true. The dragon's entire body—from its wings, to its claws, to its tail—sparkled in a way reserved for the most precious of all substances in the Minecraft universe. The entirety of the great beast was made from diamonds. Bacca had never seen anything like it.

"Whoa . . . cool!" said Bacca.

"Thank you . . . I think," the dragon replied bashfully.

"Well, I don't want to be rude," Bacca said, "but as dragons go, you don't seem very confident. Especially not for a dragon made out of diamonds."

"It's been a hard couple of weeks," the dragon replied sadly. "Some bad stuff has happened. Well, one bad thing. One really, really bad thing. Imagine how bad something would have to be to make a diamond dragon lose its confidence. It's *that* bad."

"That does sound bad," Bacca admitted. "But why are you bothering me about it?"

The dragon stopped hovering and perched on what was left of Bacca's bedroom wall.

"I come from somewhere far away—an entirely different server plane," it said. "It's a plane that most inhabitants of Minecraft don't know about. The creatures there are very different. For example, we have an emerald dragon and an ice dragon and even a pumpkin dragon."

Bacca thought that a dragon made out of pumpkins would be particularly fun to carve up in a fight, but he decided to keep that thought to himself.

"What do I call you?" Bacca asked.

"Dragons don't have names in the conventional sense," his visitor replied. "You may call me the Diamond Dragon, if you wish."

"Nice," Bacca said. "My axe is made out of diamonds. But I call her 'Betty.'"

"Anyhow, I'm here because the dragons of my server plane need your help," the dragon continued. "Two weeks ago, a sacred and powerful object was stolen from us, called the Dragon Orb. From it, the power and wisdom of all dragons radiates. Without it, the many dragons on my plane are lost and weakened. Our powers are draining away."

"That's lousy," Bacca said. "Do you know who took it?"

"Yes, we do," the dragon said.

"Oh," Bacca replied cheerily. "Then, problem solved, right? You're a bunch of dragons. You can disintegrate anything! Who's going to stand in your way if you want your Dragon Orb-thingy back?"

The dragon shook its enormous head—which was bigger than all of Bacca—to indicate that it was more complicated.

"The Dragon Orb was stolen by a clan of hostile creepers who call themselves The Creep," the dragon explained. "They're bright purple and they live in a magic fortress at the edge of the server. Without the Dragon Orb, we are powerless to penetrate their fortress. There is normally a door inside, but they have placed a magical barrier in front of it."

"That isn't very nice of them," Bacca said.

The Diamond Dragon continued: "We don't know why they stole our Dragon Orb—or what they plan to do with it—but when they took it, they left something behind. It's a riddle. We think."

"A riddle?" Bacca asked.

The enormous dragon nodded.

"We all knew immediately when the Dragon Orb was taken," the dragon said. "We could *feel* it. And when we looked where it should have been, we found a mycelium block with writing on it in a crooked, creeper hand. It said: 'To open the lock, bring us the key.'"

"What does that mean?" Bacca asked.

"We . . . erm . . . were kind of hoping *you* could figure that out," said the Diamond Dragon.

"What?" answered Bacca. "I'm a crafter, not a . . . riddle-solver-guy."

The dragon looked at Bacca seriously.

"I think that crafting *is* the only way to solve this riddle . . . and the other riddles that I fear may lie beyond," it said seriously. "Dragons cannot craft. We can only destroy. And the loss of the Dragon Orb has diminished our powers to do even that."

"I see," Bacca said, considering the situation.

"Come with me to our server plane," begged the dragon. "Let me show you the strange barrier that The Creep has created. It may be that solving this riddle is the challenge you have been preparing your whole life for, through all that crafting . . . without even knowing it."

Bacca thought carefully. A new challenge was always tempting. But this sounded like a big project, and possibly a dangerous one. Something told him he needed to proceed carefully.

"What do I get if I do this?" Bacca asked, raising a hairy eyebrow.

The dragon smiled. Bacca had never seen a dragon smile. It was kind of terrifying.

"You mentioned a diamond axe just now . . ." the dragon said confidently. "What if I told you that there was a crafting material on my server plane that was even more powerful, even stronger than diamond? And that you could craft things out of it?"

"I'd say I'd like to see that for myself," Bacca said.

"Well then," the Diamond Dragon said. "What are we waiting for? Jump onto my back, and I'll take you to my plane. If you can solve the creepers' riddles and get back the Orb, then this entirely new crafting material will be yours!"

Again, Bacca considered carefully. He already had so much. A castle full of the finest things that could be crafted (well, the castle was minus a roof, now, but that could be fixed easily). Legions of fans waiting anxiously for his next creation. All the yummy raw fish you could eat.

But a talking dragon—a talking dragon in trouble, no less—was something new and exciting. And the promise of a new crafting material? It was too much to turn down.

"I'll do it!" Bacca cried, and leapt up onto the dragon's back.

Bacca braced himself as he landed, expecting to take damage or even to be flung into space. (As he flew through the air toward the dragon, it occurred to Bacca that this could all be some sort of prank designed by one of his enemies, just to make him jump onto a dragon and disintegrate.)

But no.

Thump.

Bacca landed soundly on the dragon's back. He did not disintegrate or take damage. It was surprisingly comfortable for being made out of something as hard as diamonds.

"Ooh, it's nice up here," Bacca said. "I could just take a nap while you do all the flying."

"I advise holding on instead," the dragon said, and began beating its enormous wings.

The dragon rose high into the sky and Bacca rose with it. They flew out over the giant glistening ocean on the other side of Bacca's castle. The Overworld flew by below. Bacca could smell the sea—and, he thought, all the yummy raw fish—and feel the wind in his fur. His three-piece suit ruffled dramatically in the breeze. It was very exciting!

"Yee-haw!" cried Bacca.

"Excuse me?" said the dragon.

"Sorry . . . that just seemed like a good thing to say at a time like this," Bacca clarified.

"Oh," the dragon said. "Then go ahead."

"Yee-haw!" Bacca cried again.

The dragon seemed amused.

Far on the horizon was a tiny speck that could be easily mistaken for a block of snow or ice. It hovered high in the sky above the seemingly endless ocean. The dragon headed toward it, going faster and faster, gaining speed with every flap.

"Is it far?" Bacca shouted into the dragon's sparkling diamond ear.

"Do you see that dot up ahead?" the dragon replied.

Bacca did.

"That's the entrance to my server plane," the dragon said.

Together they flew closer and closer to the strange hovering block. As they drew close, it seemed to expand before Bacca's eyes, and he suddenly grew nervous, wondering what would happen when they reached it. Would they crash into it? Was this dragon going to splatter him all over the place? Bacca was acutely aware that diamonds were much stronger than fur and skin and all the other stuff that he was made of. What if the dragon had forgotten that what might not hurt *him* could definitely hurt Bacca? They zoomed faster toward the block, so quickly that Bacca had no other choice but to squint his eyes and hold on tight, bracing for a potentially horrible impact. In seconds they flew directly into the smooth surface, and a great blinding flash enveloped them.

Bacca blinked his eyes quickly, waiting for his sight to return. When it did, he realized that they were somewhere entirely new.

Chapter Two

A strange landscape of bedrock spread out below Bacca. Rivers of lava crisscrossed its surface. They sent out heat that Bacca could feel even from the dragon's dizzying height. The sky above was bright blue. Clusters of stone bricks hung in the air like floating islands. Some of them had blocks of ferns and flowers, and looked altogether friendly.

Much to Bacca's relief, the Diamond Dragon carefully landed on one of these friendly-looking islands. Bacca hopped down from the dragon's back.

"I guess this place is *pretty* weird . . ." Bacca pronounced skeptically. "But I've seen weirder. Heck, I've *built* weirder."

"Oh don't worry," the dragon said. "The weirdness is just getting started."

"Why are we on this little platform?" Bacca asked. "Where's the riddle? Where are the purple creepers?"

"We'll get to that shortly," the dragon said. "But first, we're going to have to speak to a welcoming committee."

"Huh?" Bacca said.

The Diamond Dragon extended a single talon toward the sky.

"Here they come now," it said.

Three floating shapes came into view in a distant part of the sky. They gradually moved closer, and Bacca realized they were also dragons.

One was a bright sparking green, and looked to be made entirely of emerald blocks. The next was a shimmering yellow that was almost certainly gold. The final one was dark blue with streaks of gold running throughout. Bacca realize it was a dragon made entirely of lapis lazuli! Bacca had never seen anything like it.

The trio made several circles in the air, sizing up the situation. Then they descended to the platform, landing with three loud *thuds!* They did not look friendly. Bacca wasn't looking for a fight, but he had brought Betty in his inventory, and was ready to reach for it if needed.

Much to Bacca's surprise, he realized the dragons' stern, angry looks were not directed at him . . . but at the Diamond Dragon.

"Who is *this*?" the Emerald Dragon asked.

"Bacca," replied the Diamond Dragon. "He's the one I was telling you about."

Bacca noticed the Diamond Dragon sounded a little defensive.

"What's a 'Bacca'?" the Lapis Lazuli Dragon asked skeptically.

"*I'm* a Bacca," said Bacca, crossing his arms.

The Lapis Lazuli Dragon arched his eyebrows to indicate this was hardly a sufficient explanation.

"I thought we agreed we didn't need help," the Gold Dragon interrupted. "Why have you brought an outsider here?"

"Because Bacca is the greatest crafter in all the Overworld!" replied the Diamond Dragon. "He knows how to make almost anything . . . out of almost anything! If there's a way to get inside this fortress holding our orb, Bacca will be the one to find it!"

"Oh, stop it," said Bacca bashfully. "You're going to make me blush."

The Emerald Dragon still seemed unconvinced.

"It's not going to look good if word gets out about this," it whispered. "We're supposed to be dragons, after all. Dragons *never* need help!"

"It will be worse if word gets out that creepers stole the orb and we couldn't get it back," the Diamond Dragon replied.

The other dragons thought about this, and nodded in reluctant agreement.

"So, does that mean I got the job?" Bacca asked.

The Emerald Dragon snorted.

"I suppose so," it said. "But consider this your probation period."

That was good enough for Bacca. He leapt back onto the Diamond Dragon.

"Then let's go get a Dragon Orb," Bacca said. "Yee haw!"

The Emerald Dragon rolled his eyes, and the dragons took off into the air.

They flew in formation across the strange plane. Bacca saw more unusual sights and odd constructions . . . but it still wasn't anything he couldn't craft himself. As they flew, Bacca wondered exactly what the Diamond Dragon expected him to do, and how he could solve the creepers' strange riddle.

Whatever it was, he was sure he was about to find out.

Chapter Three

At the edge of Bacca's vision, a mountain began to appear. And what a mountain! It was grey and black and appeared to be made from a mix of stone bricks and polished granite. Its triangular base extended up into the sky . . . and just kept extending, seeming to go on forever. Its top was completely lost in the flat, square clouds that drifted by overhead.

"That's the biggest mountain I've ever seen," Bacca called to the Diamond Dragon.

"It's not a mountain," the sparkling beast replied. "That's the home base of The Creep. A special fortress where they live. We don't know where it came from, but it's always been there. It's older than us, and full of strange things."

They flew closer. The sheer immensity of the structure began to take his breath away. That, or maybe he was getting altitude sickness. They had been flying for a long time, and Bacca was more of a land-animal.

"You're not saying the creepers built it?" Bacca asked. "I mean, creepers don't build things. They destroy things. By sneaking up on you and exploding like a big bunch of jerks."

The Diamond Dragon laughed.

"No, they didn't build it," the dragon said. "But they colonized it. They spread everywhere inside. Nobody has bothered trying to get them to leave. But it has never occurred to us to pay much attention to them at all. Until now."

"Yes, everybody usually ignores this place," the Emerald Dragon quipped from his spot at the front of the squadron formation. "But The Creep changed all of that when they stole our orb!"

"It's like they *want* us to come here," agreed the Lapis Lazuli Dragon.

"We just can't figure out why," added the Gold Dragon.

They were now close enough to the towering fortress that it entirely blotted out the sun. They flew in its shadow. Tiny birds circled above.

The dragons landed at the fortress base, where a single doorway had been constructed out of blocks of dark obsidian. Past the doorway, Bacca could see a passageway that stretched deep inside. Across the front of the doorway were a series of glowing bars made out of a strange material Bacca had never seen, casting a reddish-bluish-greenish hue that seemed to change whenever he looked at it.

Bacca dismounted from the Diamond Dragon and approached the barrier. It emitted a faint hum. Bacca shrugged, and took Betty out of his inventory. He raised the axe high above his head, and gave the nearest glowing bar a mighty chop. Immediately, a horrible pain coursed through his arm and he could feel himself losing health. The barrier was unbroken. It continued to glow and change colors. Bacca had not damaged it at all.

The dragons started laughing.

"Don't you think we already tried that sort of thing?" the Emerald Dragon said with a guffaw.

"Yeah, really," said the Gold Dragon.

"Are you absolutely *sure* this guy was worth all the trouble to bring here?" said the Lapis Lazuli one.

Bacca tried to think seriously about the problem before him. There had to be a way in. What could it be?

"How does the riddle go?" Bacca asked. "The riddle they left when they took your orb?"

The Diamond Dragon cleared his throat and spoke the words once more:

"To open the lock, bring us the key."

Bacca stroked his hairy chin and thought. He stared at the strange latticework of glowing bars that blocked off the creepers' stronghold. He carefully examined the different ways that they interlaced and connected.

Then a thought struck him. Bacca walked over to the dragons. From his inventory he produced a set of fine stone, iron, and diamond pickaxes.

"Are there any good places to mine around here?" Bacca asked.

The dragons looked at one another.

"Yes, of course," said the Diamond Dragon. "Lots and lots of them. Why?"

Bacca smiled.

"I need you to take me to the deepest, darkest place that you know," he said.

The dragons looked at one another again.

Then they nodded.

From a secret opening high atop their towering fortress, a group of bright-purple creepers known as The Creep saw the strange, hairy creature jump back atop the Diamond Dragon and fly out of sight.

There was a moment of uncomfortable silence.

"That's him?" one of the creepers said. "That hairy, fishy-smelling thing is Bacca? *The* Bacca?"

He was speaking in Creeper, the creeper's natural tongue. It was very much like the language that most everyone in Minecraft used to communicate, but much, much quieter.

"Apparently it is," said another creeper. "I thought he'd be taller. And have a nicer suit."

"Not so fast, you two," said another one. "You haven't seen him craft anything yet. That's what's important. Everything else is secondary."

"Like being tall?" added another.

"*Yes, like being tall!*" the creeper clarified angrily, with such force that for a moment it was almost—*almost*—audible to a human ear.

"Why did they leave?" one of the creepers wondered. "They just flew away."

"You know what he has to do," another creeper said. "What would you do if you were him?"

"I'd go find a mine," said the other creeper.

The creepers exchanged a meaningful look with their perfectly square eyes.

"Do you really think our plan is going to work?" one of the creepers muttered. He said this to no one in particular. As in all things, The Creep formulated their nefarious acts collectively.

The success of their plan, they all knew, would depend entirely on what Bacca did next.

The dragons flew Bacca to a giant opening that ran like a scar across the floor of their world.

"That's a mine?" Bacca asked sarcastically. "It looks like something that was left over after an earthquake."

"It's a giant hole in the ground where you can mine stuff," the Diamond Dragon replied. "If that's not a mine, I don't know what is."

The dragon had a point.

They landed next to the ragged opening, and Bacca hopped off. Then he crept forward to explore.

What he wanted very much to avoid was falling into very deep holes while mining and having to dig steps to get out again. It didn't happen often, but when it did—boy was it annoying! Peering into the dark depths below, Bacca tried to assess the terrain, and gauge the likelihood of this happening. There were blocks of dirt and stone and ore, and even obsidian. Lava flowed here and there, but there were also rivers of water. The pathway down looked jagged and confusing. Bacca decided just to jump in and hope for the best.

Before he could make his leap, Bacca heard a flapping sound that made him pause. He turned and saw all but the Diamond Dragon flying away.

"Where are your friends going?" Bacca asked.

"They have . . . important dragon business," the Diamond Dragon said. "But don't worry. They'll definitely be back."

"Are you in trouble with the other dragons for bringing me here?" Bacca asked. He had never been a person to avoid bringing up a sensitive issue.

"Um . . ." the dragon hesitated. "Let's just say that it will be really, really good for me if you can get our orb back. And really bad if you don't."

"Can I meet the Pumpkin Dragon if I get the orb back?" Bacca asked. "I really want to meet the Pumpkin Dragon."

"I suppose so," the Diamond Dragon said. ". . . and any other dragons you like . . . *if* you get the orb back."

That was all he needed to hear.

Bacca leapt into the crevasse in front of him, tumbling down into the inky blackness below.

chapter four

Bacca lit a torch.

Then, after looking around at the immense size of the hole around him, he combined some sticks and pieces of coal in his pack to make about twenty more. The place was enormous. Bacca realized it was going to be a very big job.

Once he had the torches in hand, he began to mine the craggy cave walls around him. He wasn't completely sure his plan would work—he didn't even want to *tell* the Diamond Dragon what his plan was yet—but he knew he would need quite a bit of obsidian for it.

Suddenly, Bacca stopped. Had he heard something, he wondered? Perhaps, a high-pitched, shrieking sound?

Uh oh. That was *never* good.

Bacca tossed a torch down the dark shaft ahead of him. It illuminated the walls as it flew, and came to a rest on the rocky ground. It revealed several sets of small red eyes. They seemed to be looking directly at him.

Cave spiders. Bacca had faced them many times before. Usually they were just an annoying nuisance . . . but they were also the only creature that could crawl up the sides of walls and come at you from all directions. Also, things seemed to be a little different in this server plane. Bacca didn't know if these spiders would pose any special challenges, but he decided the best thing to do was prepare for the worst.

Bacca put away his pickaxes and drew Betty from his inventory. Then he quickly donned his suit of enchanted diamond armor. The spiders edged closer. There must have been twenty of them, maybe thirty. Their breath radiated an evil green poison exhaust. (And because spiders breathe through their abdomens—not their mouths—this made their undersides glow green, which made the sight even creepier!)

Bacca didn't relish beating up on cave spiders, but they were annoying when you were trying to mine. It was also annoying when they tried to kill you.

"Hey, spiders," Bacca shouted, raising Betty high above his head, where it sparkled brilliantly in the torchlight. "We don't have to do this. Why don't you guys head the other way down the passage, and we'll forget we ever saw each other?"

The spiders did not take Bacca's advice. Instead, they moved closer and made more screeching sounds. Their little red eyes glowed. Their fangs oozed poison. They began to rock back and forth aggressively, preparing to strike.

"Oh well," said Bacca with a grin. "Don't say I didn't give you a chance to call it off!"

The first wave of spiders sprang at Bacca. Their jaws hungrily reached for him as they threw themselves forward across the floor of the mine. Bacca began to swing his axe.

"Don't—"
Chop!
"—say—"
Chop!
"—I—"
Chop!
"—didn't—"
Chop!
"—give—"
Chop!
"—you—"
Chop!
"—a—"
Chop!
"—chance!"

Bacca paused. Little bits of spider-limb were now smashed all over the cavern walls. Some of the legs even scuttled around on their own, or twitched a bit before finally going still. The remains of six or seven spiders—Bacca lost count—lay splattered all around him.

But a new wave advanced on Bacca from out of the darkness.

"Really?" Bacca said. "You just saw what happened to *these* guys. You *were* paying attention, right?"

The spiders refused to answer, and scuttled forward aggressively. Bacca raised his diamond axe once more. He knew what he had to do.

Back at the top of the crevasse, the Diamond Dragon leaned forward with an expression of concern on his face. He could not see into the dark depths where Bacca was presumably mining, but he could definitely *hear* that something was going on down there. And what he heard was beginning to make him worry. The dragon cupped one taloned hand to his ear and leaned over the craggy opening below. The "click-clack" of the pickaxe had suddenly stopped. Then it had been replaced by the sound of things being hacked into very tiny bits.

"Um . . . hello?" the dragon called tentatively. Then he summoned more confidence and roared: "Bacca? Helllooooooo?"

For a moment there was no response—nothing except the continual chopping. Then the Diamond Dragon heard Bacca's voice. The master crafter sounded a little out of breath.

"He-Hello?" Bacca called.

"Erm, is everything all right down there?" the dragon called back. "I don't hear any more mining."

After a moment, Bacca replied.

"That . . . because . . . I'm . . . killing . . . *spiders*!"

The dragon looked left and right, then blinked repeatedly.

"Oh," the dragon said, thinking. "Do you need any help with that?"

"No . . . I've . . . got . . . it . . . under . . . *control*!" Bacca's voice came back.

"Ah" the dragon said—a little puzzled, but willing to take Bacca at his word. "Very good. Just let me know if I can do anything to be of assistance."

After a moment, and more chopping sounds, Bacca's voice came back.

"Okay . . . I . . . *will!!!*"

The battle was over. Bacca put Betty back in his inventory pack and wiped the sweat from his furry forehead. All around him were the bodies of spiders that had decided not to listen to reason. Their glowing red eyes slowly extinguished like embers in a dying fire.

Whew, thought Bacca. It was hard enough to fight spiders. It was even harder to do it when a dragon wants to have a conversation with you at the same time.

Bacca looked up toward the opening of the crevasse where the Diamond Dragon lingered, and thought about their previous conversation. It sounded like the Diamond Dragon had taken a real risk in inviting him here. Apparently, the beast would be in some kind of trouble if they didn't get the Dragon Orb back. Because of this, Bacca decided not to have any hard feelings against the dragon for interrupting him while he was trying to fight spiders. The dude was under a lot of pressure.

With this in mind, he felt more determined than ever to make his plan succeed.

Bacca lit another torch and looked around for any additional spiders lurking at the edge of his vision. He didn't see any. Good.

In that case, it was time to get back to work.

For what seemed like many hours, the Diamond Dragon waited patiently at the top of the crevasse. To pass the time, he looked at the large square clouds floating by and reflected—for the umpteenth time—on just how much trouble he was going to be in if Bacca's plan failed. He imagined all the punishments the other dragons would devise for him. Dragons could be quite creative where punishments were concerned. The Diamond Dragon wasn't looking forward to it.

The sound of Bacca's approach shook him back to reality.

"Hey there," Bacca said, hopping up out of the crevasse.

"You're back!" said the Diamond Dragon. "Did you get what you needed? You still haven't told me why we're here."

Bacca looked exhausted from fighting and mining. The dragon could also tell that his inventory was now very, very full.

"Can you fly me back to the fortress where the creepers live?" Bacca asked. "I warn you, I'll be heavier now. Got a lot of blocks with me."

"I think I can manage it," said the dragon. "I *am* a dragon, you know."

Bacca hopped aboard and the dragon took to the skies. They flew back over the strange landscape until the immense triangular fortress loomed in the distance. Down below, a group of dragons had gathered at the fortress door. Bacca wondered if the Pumpkin Dragon was among them.

"What are they doing?" Bacca asked.

"They're here to see what you're going to do," the dragon said. "Word gets around."

Bacca smiled to himself. He wasn't nervous. He had a feeling his plan would work.

The Diamond Dragon landed in front of the immense creeper citadel. Bacca faced a new round of skepticism from the dragons who had gathered to watch.

"*That's* what we're depending on to get the Dragon Orb back?" said an Ice Dragon rather rudely. "That hairy thing?"

Bacca considered how satisfying it might be to throw some torches at the Ice Dragon. Just to see what would happen. Then he thought better of it, and turned his attention back to the riddle.

As the gathering of dragons looked on, Bacca began pulling blocks of obsidian out of his inventory and stacking them into place. He was building something, but *what* he was building was not immediately obvious to the dragony audience. Every so often, Bacca stopped what he was doing to peer over at the fortress with its strange glowing bars. Then he went back to stacking the dark squares of obsidian together.

"What do you think he's making?" one dragon murmured.

"It's like a long tube," said another. "Except it's got pointy bits at one end, and the other end is like a flat circle."

"That shape seems awfully familiar," said a third. "I just can't quite put my talons on it."

Bacca worked and worked. He'd built more complicated structures before, sure. But this one was especially challenging because he knew he had to get every part of it—especially what the dragons were calling the "pointy bits"—exactly right. The finished product was several times larger than he was, but not quite the size of a dragon. When he decided it was finally complete, he stepped away and wiped the sweat from his brow.

"There," Bacca said. "It's done. Now all that's left is for you dragons to put it in the lock. And turn it."

"Oh!" several of the dragons seemed to say in unison. "It's a key! How didn't we see that earlier?"

This was true.

Bacca had crafted a giant key out of obsidian. It looked perfectly tailored to fit into the opening at the base of the creeper's fortress. The teeth of the key would go in the spaces between the glowing bars.

"Yes," Bacca said. "That riddle the creepers left you was literal. They were asking for a physical key. Somebody just had to build it. So I did."

The dragons looked at each other.

"Diamond Dragon, this was your idea," someone in the herd of dragons said. "Maybe you should be the one to see if it works."

The Diamond Dragon looked over at the giant obsidian key, then at Bacca.

Bacca gave him a wink.

The Diamond Dragon approached the key and used its incredible strength to lift it.

"Hrrrgh," the dragon said, straining. He slowly moved it to the opening of the creeper fortress, then pushed it inside. It fit perfectly.

The dragons' jaws dropped in amazement. Bacca found himself looking at a lot of pointy sharp teeth all at once.

"Now turn it," Bacca said. "You are familiar with how keys work, aren't you?"

The Diamond Dragon gave Bacca an annoyed look and gripped the key's handle. The key began to turn. There was a low, grating sound of obsidian and stone scraping. The key rotated until there was a loud "click" noise.

Suddenly, the glow from the strange bars in the entrance ceased. The Diamond Dragon removed the key. When he did, they saw that the bars had disappeared. The way ahead was clear. The dragons peered cautiously into the darkness beyond.

"He's done it!" cried one dragon.

"That wasn't so complicated," said another. "I mean, a key? *I* could have thought of that."

"Oh yeah?" said the first dragon. "Then why didn't you?"

The Diamond Dragon cast Bacca an expression of thanks and relief. Bacca was glad he had figured out how to get inside the fortress, but he had a sinking feeling that his work wasn't over yet. Bacca lit a torch and headed into the fortress. The dragons cautiously followed.

"I wish we could just knock this place down," one of the dragons mumbled. "That's the first thing we'll do when we get the orb back."

The corridor opened into a huge clearing with a very high ceiling. Very, very high. Higher than most castles. So high the dragons could fly around inside, if they wanted to. There were openings in the ceiling where shafts of light penetrated. Bacca saw indistinct movement in the shadows. Was it something hostile? He prepared to draw Betty and face down any creepers who might be waiting to explode.

Then a cry echoed across the walls.

"Baaaaa."

Other, similar noises joined it. Several of the tones actually sounded curious.

"Baaaa?"

"What is that?" the Diamond Dragon asked.

"It's sheep," Bacca replied, taking his hand off his weapon. "Lots and lots of sheep. See them over there, on the other side of the clearing? They were just hanging out here eating grass. I think we scared them."

"Do you see the Dragon Orb anywhere?" one of the dragons asked from the rear.

"Well, you haven't told me what it looks like," Bacca replied snarkily. "But no, I don't. Unless it's behind a sheep."

Then Bacca spied something that made him pause.

"What did you say the riddle was written on?" Bacca asked. "The riddle they left when they took the orb?"

"A mycelium block," said the Diamond Dragon. "Why? Do you see—"

Then he saw it. They all did. A mycelium block with writing on it, waiting for them in the center of the giant clearing.

"Oh no," said the Diamond Dragon. "I don't even want to look. Is it another riddle? Why won't they just give us back our magic orb?!"

"Well, they *are* called creepers," said Bacca. "As in, they're creeps. Plus, they creep up on you. I guess it works on lots of levels. But c'mon, let's go see what it says!"

Bacca and the dragons crowded around the mycelium block. Bacca help up his torch and read the inscription out loud.

The floor here is thick with graves; a zombie's delight.
In an hour, the horde will rise.
The likes of it, you have never seen.
When they come, one alone must survive.
That person may not leave until the walking dead do.
Only then will the way open.
How will you use your time?

There was a moment of silence as Bacca and the dragons pondered over the riddle. Then there was a moment of *loudness*!

It was sudden and jarring, like the shifting of many feet on a gravel walkway. Or a rainstick. Or actual rain. Bacca looked toward the direction of the loud sound, and saw that an hourglass was affixed high on the wall of the room. As if by magic—or, more probably, *by* magic—the sands had begun to trickle through. Bacca watched the grains fall. He reckoned that he likely had an hour until the top part of the glass was empty.

"Okaaaay," the Diamond Dragon said. "That's certainly strange. What do we do now?"

"Hmm," Bacca said. "I need to think about this one for a second. Could you guys give me some privacy?"

"Right," the Diamond Dragon said, pleased to have some direction. "Everybody out. You heard him. There's another riddle, and he's not going to solve it with all of you guys bothering him."

The rest of the dragons grudgingly headed back outside. Soon, their thunderous footfalls died away and all Bacca could hear was the sand wooshing through the hourglass.

Only the Diamond Dragon remained.

"This is just a guess," Bacca began. "But I think the riddle is saying that when the hourglass runs out, there are going to be a whole bunch of zombies in this room. And I mean a *whole* bunch. Also according to the riddle, I have an hour to get ready. And I have to be in here alone. And I can't leave."

"How much obsidian do you have left in your inventory?" the Diamond Dragon asked with a worried look.

"Zero," Bacca said. "I mined just enough to make the key. I'm very precise."

"So what are you going to do?" the dragon asked.

In the distance, one of the sheep went "Baaaa."

"Oh," Bacca said, "I think I can improvise."

Chapter Five

There was great consternation in the headquarters of the creepers. (Consternation is like being worried, except it's done much quieter.)

"He made the key!" one of the creepers nervously observed. "He got through! He even let the dragons come in with him!"

"But that didn't involve much danger," another of the creepers said. "That was just making a key. How much of a test was it, really?"

"He had to go to Spider Canyon to mine that much obsidian," another pointed out. "It's got dangerous spiders. And other things, too. *I* don't even like to go there, and I'm a creeper!"

"Maybe you've got a point," said the previous creeper. "But I think we can agree this next challenge will be much, much more dangerous."

"Is that a good thing?" asked another creeper. "Or a bad thing?"

"Depends on how you look at it," answered another. "If he doesn't survive then . . . well, he wasn't the right crafter to begin with."

"So . . ." said one of the creepers, straining to think as hard as he could. "We want it to be very dangerous . . . but we also want him to survive?"

There was a general murmuring of agreement throughout the creeper ranks.

"Come on," said one of them. "I want to go down and see what he does! How he solves the problem! We can watch him through the skylights."

"Ooh, that sounds exciting!" said another.

"Me first!" shouted another.

The creepers scrambled to the openings in the roof and looked down at Bacca as he planned his next move.

"Really?" said the Diamond Dragon. "I have to leave, too?"

Bacca nodded.

"If you want me to solve this riddle, you do," he answered. "Those are the rules."

The Diamond Dragon began to slink back outside. Then he turned and said: "Thank you, by the way."

"Huh?" Bacca said.

"If you hadn't figured out we needed a *literal* key, I'd be in big trouble with the other dragons now," the Diamond Dragon said. "You really saved my reputation. So . . . thanks."

"I haven't saved anything yet," Bacca answered. "Thank me when we get the Dragon Orb back. Now—and I say this with all respect—*please leave* so I can get to work."

"Sorry!" said the Diamond Dragon, and lurched back out of the enormous room.

When he heard the last of the dragon's footsteps fade into the distance, Bacca took out his pickaxe. He had a theory about the lumpy ground all around him. He wanted to test it out.

Bacca raised a pickaxe and struck at the spot directly below him. Once! Twice! Thrice!

Crack!

The ground parted, and Bacca saw just what he was afraid he might see. A ghoulish zombie rose up out of the earth. Its fingernails were long like claws, and its teeth gnashed violently.

For a fraction of an instant, Bacca could have sworn that the zombie made an expression that said: "Aren't we starting this just a tad early?"

But as soon as it had come, the expression passed, and the zombie gave Bacca a look that was more typical for zombies: that it would very much like to eat Bacca's brain!

"I thought so," Bacca said with a frown, and quickly switched over to Betty. The shining diamond blade flew through the air. With a few quick whacks, Bacca sent the zombie tumbling back to the ground in separate parts.

"The entire floor of this place has zombies underneath it!" Bacca cried out loud, even though there was no one else in the room to hear him. "That's why it was so lumpy!"

The creepers had placed these zombies underneath the floor of the room. Somehow, they were connected to the hourglass.

Bacca had a bad feeling that when the hourglass on the wall ran out of sand, all of them were going to pop up out of the ground and go on the hunt.

For him. Bacca also understood that the tablet said he wasn't allowed to leave. He had to use only what was available to him in this room. Faced with such a challenge, Bacca did the only thing he could think of. He reached into his inventory and pulled out a pair of shiny metal shears.

"Here, sheepy sheepy sheepy," he called.

The sheep were scattered all around the room. Now they began to look at him curiously.

Bacca knew you got more wool from a sheep if you sheared it than if you just killed it, so he was careful to spare each of them. He went about his work quickly, sprinting from sheep to sheep and shearing each one. A few of the sheep tried to run away.

"Come back here, you silly sheep!" Bacca cried as he ran after them. "I don't know if zombies eat sheep, but do you really want to find out? Believe me, when I get done, you'll be glad I'm doing this. Now, stop running and hold still!"

Shearing all the sheep took longer than Bacca would have liked, but he had a feeling he would need all of the wool for his plan to work. There was no other resource to use, and digging in the ground would only release more zombies!

Bacca scanned the interior of the enormous clearing and decided on a spot against one of the walls. The natural bedrock would help him, Bacca decided, and zombies didn't live in walls . . . as far as he knew. (And at this point, Bacca realized he was going to have to take some chances!)

Using the wool blocks, Bacca began to build a floor and foundation. Soon, the grey blocks formed a large circle against the high bedrock wall. Then he started to build stairs, outer walls, inner walls, and a series of platforms. He was building a small castle, and it was going to be made *entirely* out of wool.

Bacca had never tried this before, but he guessed that a wool block would keep out a zombie just as well as a block made of something else. As he worked away, the sheared sheep sometimes wandered over to stare at him. They appeared to be curious. And also a bit chilly.

"You could help if you wanted to," Bacca said. But the sheep were not helpful. They just looked at him and wandered around. Even though they were just standing there being annoying, Bacca took pity and made sure all of the sheep were safely inside the first floor of the castle before he walled it shut.

The sand in the hourglass was about to run out. Bacca decided he would have to switch gears mid-craft. Instead of a tower, the wool castle would have to have something more like a platform. This castle wasn't going to win any awards for design, but it would hopefully be strong enough to keep out the zombies, which was all he really cared about.

Bacca crafted the platform and found he still had a few blocks of wool to spare. He used them to reinforce places along the wall where the wool looked a bit thin. Then the last perfectly square grain of sand fell to the bottom of the hourglass, and the room went silent. Bacca climbed his fortification's wooly stairs and stood atop the platform. He looked down at the floor of the clearing below. For a moment, all was still.

Then he started to hear a new sound. It was a low moan. Then another moan joined it, and another after that.

Just as Bacca had feared, a ravenous horde of zombies began rising from the floor. A grisly hand poked its way up through the topsoil and grasped aggressively at the air. Then another. Then a gleaming zombie skull emerged. What flesh remained was covered with wriggling worms. Ew! This pattern repeated itself throughout the floor of the room. The zombies pushed aside the earth and popped out, ready to cause mayhem and eat people. Or, more specifically, to eat *Bacca*.

He tried to count them. Fifty? A hundred? Two hundred? He'd never seen so many zombies. They just kept coming! Soon, the mob of walking dead was pressing hard against the outer walls of Bacca's castle. It was a sea of moaning monsters, like something from his worst nightmares! The zombies looked up at Bacca hungrily, and pawed the wool in frustration.

But they did not make any progress. The wool held firm.

His plan was going to work!

"Poor old zombies," Bacca said. "They can't read. They can't cooperate. They can't even get through wool. All they can do is try to eat your brains. Well, you're not eating anybody's brains *today*, zombies! Not if I have anything to do with it!"

From down on the first floor of the wool castle, Bacca heard a loud "Baaaa."

"Oh, was that a 'Thank you?'" Bacca said sarcastically. "You're welcome, I guess. Silly sheep!"

The zombies moaned and shrieked and pressed against the wall of the wool castle, but they couldn't get inside. The well-crafted walls stood strong. After a while, the zombies started looking a little frustrated. Then Bacca saw something he'd never seen before; a zombie gave up! It lay its body back down on the ground and scooped the earth back over itself. Soon, the block that held the zombie looked as though it had never been disturbed in the first place. Then another zombie did the same thing. Another followed, and soon the rest of the horde began to catch on. One big zombie slumber party was happening right in front of Bacca's eyes. One by one, the creatures left the walls of the wool castle and found their original places back underneath the soil.

"This isn't how zombies are supposed to act," Bacca joked nervously, relieved that the danger had passed. "You guys are going to be in trouble if the head zombie finds out!"

Bacca was pleased. His plan had worked. When the last of the zombies had buried itself back underground, and enough time had passed that it seemed safe to assume their retreat wasn't a trick, Bacca hopped down to the first floor of the wool castle. He knocked down a few of the wool blocks and let the sheep back outside.

"Silly sheep," Bacca said a final time, because they really were quite silly.

No sooner had Bacca done this, than the blocks on the far side of the giant room began to move, as if by magic. There was a loud grating noise, and a new pathway opened before him. He had solved the riddle!

Bacca did not advance to the mysterious new opening, but instead walked back outside to where the dragons were waiting patiently.

"It's done," Bacca told them. "I built a castle out of wool. Zombies came up, but I was safe. The zombies went away, and then a new door opened. But no orb. I don't think we're out of the woods yet."

The many varieties of dragon murmured to one another that this was extraordinary.

"A castle out of wool?" said the Emerald Dragon. "How did you know to do *that*?"

"I just did," Bacca replied. "I'm Bacca. I figure stuff out."

The Emerald Dragon narrowed its eyes a little, but did not question Bacca's expertise.

"Let's see what's in the new room," the Lapis Lazuli Dragon said.

"Ooh, let's!" said the Gold Dragon.

Bacca crossed his arms.

"Not so fast," Bacca said. "I don't know what we're going to find going forward, but I'm the one doing all of the crafting. I need to work without being interrupted. So I think you need to let me do this alone."

The Emerald Dragon lifted his eyebrow suspiciously.

"What makes you think we should trust you?" it said.

"You *guys,* come *on,*" Bacca replied in frustration. "What am I going to do? Steal the Dragon Orb for myself? What would I use it for? I'm a crafter, not a dragon."

"I guess you have a point," the Emerald Dragon relented.

"Okay," the Gold Dragon chimed in. "But please. Be *really* careful with it. It's super important to us."

"Yeah, I got that much," Bacca said. "But also, you really do need to tell me what it looks like. How will I know it when I see it?"

"That's easy," the Diamond Dragon said. "It's a big glowing ball with the letter 'd' on it."

"Capital, or lower case?" Bacca said.

The dragons were clearly puzzled and did not reply.

"Never mind," Bacca said. "I'm sure I can wing it. And one more thing. Until I come back, I want you all to be nice to the Diamond Dragon. Apparently he was the only one who believed I was the right man for this job, and he went to a lot of trouble to bring me here. So the rest of you should be polite and show him some respect, okay?"

The Diamond Dragon blushed, its sparkling cheeks taking on a rosy glow. It said nothing, but Bacca could tell the great beast appreciated his words.

The other dragons mumbled something about being nicer to the Diamond Dragon in the future.

"Good," said Bacca. "Now with that settled, I'm headed back inside. When you see me again, I'll have your dragon orb-thingy."

And with that, Bacca turned on his heels and bravely stormed back inside the fortress!

chapter six

Bacca strode through the large chamber where his wool castle still towered. He regarded it fondly as he passed. It wasn't going to make the cover of *Better Minecraft Homes and Gardens,* but it had certainly served its purpose. Bacca slowed his pace, lit a torch, and then proceeded through the mysterious door that had opened in the far side of the chamber. The way ahead was dark and forbidding. Even the curious sheep had decided to stay away from it.

Bacca walked through the door and down the corridor beyond. It was not very large.

"Good thing I made those dragons stay behind," Bacca said. "They'd never have fit in here."

The corridor stretched in a perfectly straight line, and suddenly terminated in a large door. The door was made of unassuming blocks of polished diorite, and had a golden handle. The border of the door was trimmed in redstones. Bacca listened, and found he could hear sounds coming from the other side of the door. It was running water (which had the unanticipated effect of making him wonder hungrily if this might mean the presence of fish!).

Then, set into the wall beside the door, Bacca found the final item he was expecting. It was another mycelium block with writing carved into it. He approached it and began to read:

The resident of this room doesn't like to show his face.
But you must paint it for him
If you ever hope to succeed.
Everything you need for this task, you will surely find within.

"Hmm," said Bacca. "That's a weird one."

He gripped the golden handle and gave it a turn. The polished diorite door swung open. Through the doorway was a very strange room indeed. Its defining feature was a large, deep pool of crystal clear water. The borders of the pool were surrounded by ferns, lily pads, vines, and flowers of all shapes and sizes. There was a ring of sand surrounding the pool like a little beach. A waterfall cascaded down from the ceiling of the room and splashed into the pool. Instead of stone, the room's floor featured tall grass and coarse dirt. The walls were wet mossy cobblestone. The room was illuminated by a series of torches.

Bacca did not see any doors or passageways leading away from this room. He also did not see any people or creatures inside. But there was a wooden frame hanging on one of the walls. It was rectangular and very large. The more Bacca looked at it, the more Bacca thought it looked just the right shape to hold a canvas for a painting.

Bacca entered the room and shut the polished diorite door quietly. Nothing in the room looked particularly dangerous, but he wanted to tread carefully.

He walked to the large pool with its waterfall cascading down from the heights above. Where was the water coming from? Bacca took a torch and threw it as high as he could. The room seemed to have no ceiling. The water streamed from an endless darkness rising above him.

"Innnnnteresting," Bacca said with a smile.

Bacca looked down into the pool. Several fish were swimming in the clear blue water, and a mob of squid was silently bobbing up and down.

Bacca stared at the fish, his stomach growling hungrily.

"Maybe it'll be okay if I eat just one . . ." he said.

He reached down toward the water, ready to pluck out one of the shimmering fish and pop it into his mouth. But before his hand could touch the water, something made him stop. Bacca realized there was something at the bottom of the pool. He squinted through the rippling water and looked more closely. It was a cave. There, at the very bottom of the water, a dark, forbidding opening was waiting to be explored.

Bacca backed away from the pool and walked around the rest of the room, looking for any sign of life. Nothing moved. There was only the flickering of the torches along the walls. Bacca certainly didn't see the "resident" that the inscription on the mycelium block had referenced.

He cupped his paws to his mouth to make a megaphone.

"Hello!" Bacca shouted. "Is anybody here?"

There was no response at first—only the splashing of the waterfall.

Then Bacca heard a voice. It was low and sounded like stone grating on stone. It seemed to be coming from somewhere very far away.

"Hello?" it said nervously.

"Hi there!" Bacca said.

There was another pause.

"Who are you?" the voice said. It still sounded scared.

"I'm Bacca," Bacca said. "Don't worry. I'm friendly. Generally."

Bacca remembered the wording of the riddle.

"I'm here to paint your portrait," Bacca said. "Doesn't that sound nice?"

"No," the distant voice responded.

Bacca twirled all around the room, but could not see who was addressing him. Did the voice come from the same place that the water did? The endless ceiling of darkness above?

"Where are you?" Bacca asked. "And *who* are you?"

"My name's Bill," the voice said. "I live in the cave at the bottom of the pool."

Aha, thought Bacca. Now we're getting somewhere.

"Look, Bill, why don't you come out of the cave for just a second?" Bacca said. "I'm trying to solve this riddle. To do that, I need to see what you look like so I can paint a picture of you."

There was another very . . . long . . . pause.

The voice said: "Are you joking? Did someone put you up to this? Because I don't come out for *anybody.* Everybody knows that about me. I'm famous for it. I'm Bill, the hermit who stays in his cave."

"Sorry, I didn't know," Bacca said. "I'm a visitor. I'm not even from this server plane."

"Perfectly all right," the voice said. "No hard feelings. But I'm still not coming out."

Bacca sighed. He'd suspected there would be an unusual challenge to this riddle. Now it looked like he was right.

"Can you *describe* what you look like?" Bacca pressed. "That way, I could paint your portrait, and you wouldn't have to come out of your cave."

"No!" said Bill. "That would defeat the whole purpose of being a hermit." Then, as an afterthought, the voice added: "But I assure you, I'm good looking. Very, *very* good looking."

Bacca frowned.

"What if I gave you something in return?" Bacca asked. He rifled through his inventory. There had to be *something* this mysterious hermit wanted.

"Nope," the voice said. "Not interested. I've got everything I need already."

"Are you sure?" Bacca said. "I've got a bunch of really cool stuff! Swords, and axes, and pickaxes, and shovels . . ."

"Been there, done that already," the voice boomed back sternly. "You don't have anything I want. Now go away!"

Well that was rather rude, Bacca thought. Still, he was not about to give up. There *had* to be some way to get this mysterious "Bill" to come out of his cave just for a second. Bacca crept once again to the edge of the pool. He stared down at the cave beneath the water. Frustratingly, there was absolutely nothing to see. Bill was entirely hidden.

Then a glint of light from the torches made Bacca notice his own reflection in the surface of the pool . . . and suddenly a solution occurred to him.

Eureka, Bacca thought!

He walked a few steps away from the pool, and picked up a handful of sand.

Bacca let it run through his paws. Yes, he thought. This would do nicely.

A smile came to his lips.

It was time to start crafting.

"Oooooh! What's he doing? Let me see, let me see, let me see!"

The creepers spying on Bacca from the darkness above jostled with one another to get the best view of the action.

"He's *never* going to get Bill to come out," said one creeper confidently.

"Yeah," said another. "Bill never, ever comes out. I've been friends with Bill for ten years, and I've never seen him once!"

"But then . . . if Bill's not coming out . . . what's Bacca trying to do?" asked another creeper.

They all looked down at Bacca, curiosity spreading across their faces.

"He's really focused on the sand," one observed. "It looks like he's cooking it. Why? Is he going to eat it or something?"

"Cooking sand?" said another. "That's how you make glass."

"Why's he making glass?" asked a third. "If Bill's not coming out for something cool like a sword or a pickaxe, he's sure not coming out for a piece of glass."

The creepers watched, equal parts confused and enthralled.

"He's sure making a lot of it," one of the creepers said. "Why's he making so much?"

They watched as Bacca began to lift the sheets of glass and stack them in an ordered row against the wall.

"Is he making a big window?" one of the creepers said.

"That's a *horrible* place for a window," said another. "Just horrible."

"Yeah," said a third. "Look through it, and all you'll see is that mossy old wall. When I look out of windows, I like to see something pretty. Like a nice sunset. Or, ooh, a pretty forest."

"Wait!" another creeper interrupted, overtaken with excitement. "Now's he's adding blocks to the portrait frame!"

The other creepers looked on, equally astounded. They had, of course, left the frame there as part of the riddle. It would be where Bacca would create his portrait of Bill. But how would Bacca do that without having seen him?

As the creepers watched, Bacca mined for different blocks, and also took a liberal selection of the flowers and plants available throughout the mossy room. He took these materials and began to stack them into the wooden frame. Before long, a face began to take shape.

"That doesn't look like Bill at all!" one of the creepers said. "And I've actually seen him! Well, I mean, not personally. But someone *told* me what he looks like. I have it on very strong authority . . ."

The face Bacca had constructed inside the frame looked very silly. It had a crooked nose of prismarine, a mouth made of coarse dirt that was uneven on one side, and eyes made from flowers. Large stone eyebrows gave it a stern expression. The ears were made of dead bushes, and the hair was made from bright green lily pads.

As the creepers looked on, Bacca stepped back from the frame to admire his work. He held up his thumb like a painter, and looked past it at what he had created on the canvas. His lips curled into a grin. Bacca appeared very pleased.

"He *can't* be finished," one of the creepers sputtered. "That's the worst painting I ever saw. And I once went to a zombie pigman art show!"

"Yes, that looks truly awful," another creeper agreed. "A complete failure, artistic or otherwise."

"Maybe we made this riddle too difficult," said a third creeper. "That's a pity. I thought for sure Bacca would be able to figure it out. Now it looks like he's just guessing."

The creepers all agreed that Bacca's approach to the riddle had taken a disappointing turn.

But far beneath them, Bacca strode confidently back to the edge of the pool with the gait of a man who has the situation completely under control. He looked down into the water's crystalline blue depths and smiled. He knew something the creepers did not: that everything was going according to plan.

"Hello there!" Bacca called down into the pool. "I'm all finished. Do you want to take a look?"

For a moment there was only the sound of the wooshing waterfall. Then Bill's sonorous voice reverberated up through the water.

"What are you talking about?" it said.

"Your portrait, silly," Bacca replied. "I'm done painting it. I don't mean to boast, but I believe that I got you exactly right. I really captured your essence, so to speak."

"*What?*" Bill said, confused. "That's impossible! You can't have painted my picture. You don't know what I look like. Nobody does. I'm Bill, the hermit. I live in a cave at the bottom of a pool inside the creeper fortress!!! *How can you know what I look like???*"

"I saw you the other day when you weren't looking," Bacca said. "For just a split second. It was all I needed. I've got a photographic memory."

"No!" Bill cried, but from his voice, Bacca could tell that he was suddenly unsure. "That never happened!"

"Just come up and see," Bacca said sweetly.

There was a long pause.

"No," the deep voice finally concluded. "If I come up, then you *will* see what I look like."

"Seriously, you're overthinking this," Bacca said. "I already know what you look like. I just made a perfect picture of you."

"No!" Bill insisted again. "That's not possible!"

Bacca could tell Bill was now agitated enough to make a mistake.

"Tell you what," Bacca said. "I'll leave the room and go back down the hallway. If I do that, there's no way I'll be able to see you. I'll be out of the room. You can come out and take a look at my portrait. Then I'll come back in a couple of minutes, and you can tell me if it's right or not. We'll never be in the same room together."

"Um . . ." Bill said, clearly considering it.

"Because I'm like ninety-nine percent sure it's completely right," Bacca said.

"*No, it's not!*" Bill boomed. "Fine! We'll do it your way. If that's what it takes for you to understand that *you're wrong.*"

Bacca smiled. He had him!

"Okay," Bacca said. "I'll leave now so you can come take a look."

Exaggerating his footsteps with giant stomps, Bacca walked back to the door.

"Heading out now," Bacca said. "I'll see you in a bit."

Bacca went through the doorway, but made certain to leave the door open behind him. He retreated far down the hallway, nearly back to the high-ceilinged clearing where his wool castle still towered. Then Bacca turned around, looked through the doorway, and squinted hard. It all came down to this. Now he would find out if his plan was going to work!

Peering back into the room with the pool, Bacca focused his eyes on the wall of glass he had built. Normally, anyone looking down the hall into the room would not be able to see the pool. And that was still true. However, Bacca's glass wall allowed him to see the reflection of the pool, and—he hoped—anybody who might come out of it.

Bacca cupped his hands to his mouth and shouted. He wasn't even sure Bill would be able to hear him at this distance, but he gave it a shot.

"Hello!" Bacca called. "I'm *waaaaay* at the other end of this tunnel! I'm, like, super far away from you! Come out now and take a look at my painting!"

Bacca waited and watched. In the reflection in the wall of glass, Bacca scanned the surface of the pool.

At first, it was motionless except for the ripples cast by the waterfall. Then Bacca saw something! A dark, wet shape began to rise out of the water. It was the top of a head . . . then an entire head! It was dark grey and square, with a bulbous nose and beady red eyes. Its ears were jagged and stuck up like knives. The mouth was very small and almost entirely covered by its nose.

Then more of the creature emerged, and Bacca was sure of it . . .

Bill was an iron golem! His skin was made from iron ingots, and he wore green ivy across his torso like a toga. Unlike most iron golems, he had a blemish on his neck—like a wart—made from a single piece of coal. Bill moved slowly and steadily up out of the pool. It was clear his red eyes were unaccustomed to the torchlight.

Bill looked around carefully for any sign of Bacca. When he was satisfied that he was alone, he walked over to the frame where Bacca's strange "portrait" rested. Bill shook his head as if to say the artist had got it completely wrong. Then he turned around and plunged back in the pool.

All this took only a few seconds, but Bacca was thrilled. It had worked! Now he had just what he needed.

"Okay!" Bacca shouted. "I'm coming back now! I hope you got a good look!"

Bacca bounded back down the corridor.

"You were *way* off," boomed Bill's deep, metallic voice. He was already back inside his aquatic cave.

"My mistake," Bacca said with a grin. But he was no longer worried. He began breaking apart the first set of blocks he had placed into the large wooden rectangle. *Smash! Smash!* Soon they were all tiny bits on the floor, and Bacca had a clean canvas to work from.

Bacca set about creating a perfect portrait of Bill. To get the texture of the golem's grey face just right, he used stone, quartz, andesite, and blocks of solid iron. Then he harvested more of the green flora that grew around the pool and used it to duplicate the green toga that dappled across Bill's body. He even found a piece of coal that would replicate the hermit's wart. As a finishing touch, Bacca took water from the pool and splashed it across his blocky painting. Soon, the golem in Bacca's painting looked dripping wet—just like Bill.

With mounting confidence, Bacca crept back over to the pool's edge.

"Hello?" he called. "Bill? Are you still there?"

"What do you want now?" Bill called back. "Can't you just leave me alone?"

"I painted a new portrait of you," Bacca said. "Wanna see it? This time, I think you'll agree it's spot-on!"

"Don't waste my time," Bill said. "You're just bluffing now."

"I'm really not," Bacca said. "If you just give me one more chance, this time I know I'll win you over."

"No," said Bill. "This conversation is over. Go away!"

"Bill?" Bacca said. "Hello? Hellooooo?"

There was no response. Bacca realized this was the silent treatment. The golem had decided to stop responding altogether. Bacca decided it was time for drastic measures.

"You have grey iron skin," Bacca said teasingly. "Your eyes are small and red, and your long nose hooks down over your tiny mouth. You wear green strands made out of plant vines. And you have a big wart on your neck made out of a piece of coal."

". . ."

There was silence, yes, but Bacca could tell it was a *tense* silence. A *meaningful* silence. Bill was thinking hard.

"How do you know that?" Bill's voice eventually boomed back. "I mean . . . I'm not saying it's right. But if it *was* right . . . how do you know? Nobody knows what I look like! How could you possibly have found out?"

"I have my ways," Bacca said, glancing over at the wall of glass. "You should come up and see for yourself. I think this second painting really gets it right. Here, I'll leave the room again. No tricks."

Bacca laughed to himself. He was, of course, full of tricks. They were what he was known for. Well, tricks and crafting.

Bacca retreated down the corridor, but kept one eye on the room behind him. Sure enough, he soon saw a dark grey iron golem rise up out of the water. It looked really annoyed.

In the reflection created by his glass wall, Bacca watched it walk over to the frame where the new portrait was displayed. Now that Bacca saw them both together, he knew for sure he'd done it. His painting was a perfect match!

"Oh no," cried Bill. "It's like looking into a mirror! It's me exactly!"

Bacca bounded back down the hallway.

"*You!*" the stone golem cried. "*You're* Bacca?"

"In the flesh," Bacca said.

The iron golem collapsed on the floor, as if suddenly overtaken by a deep depression.

"Now that somebody knows what I look like, there's no point in staying here," Bill said. "I'll have to move. Find an entirely new biome. There's no point to being a mysterious hermit if there's a big painting of you that anybody can come see."

Bacca started to feel bad for the golem.

"You don't have to leave," Bacca said. "I won't tell anybody it's you. I only did this because it was part of the riddle left by the creepers."

Bacca explained his quest to regain the dragon orb, and the riddle that he had been trying to solve.

"Those creeper jerks," said Bill. "I knew this fortress was headed downhill when they took over. Some people said having a bunch of creepers around would help keep people away. They said it could actually be good for a hermit. Shows what they know."

Then the golem put his hand on his chin, as if a thought had occurred to him.

"There's a trap door in my cave that leads down to the creeper's dungeon maze," Bill said. "I expect they wanted you to solve the riddle by going there next. That would make sense, because you'd have to be rid of me to get there."

"Thanks," Bacca said, though he didn't like the sound of a dungeon maze.

Bill sighed.

"As for me," the golem said, "I guess I'll go live in the ice wastes in the winter biome to the north. It's got great big blocky cliffs and deep chasms made out of frozen things. I'll bet it would be pretty easy to not get found up there. Although, that's what I thought about this place . . . and look how that turned out."

"There are some friendly dragons outside," Bacca told him. "I bet one of them would give you a ride if you liked."

"Thanks," said the iron golem. "I'll think about it. This is all happening so fast. I'm sad to be leaving my home—but more than that, I'm angry at the creepers. If there's anything I can ever do to help you get back at those darn creepers, just come north and find me."

"Okay," said Bacca. "I certainly will."

When the iron golem had gone, Bacca held his nose and plunged into the glistening pool of water. He swam down to the cave. It was very dark inside—and of course he couldn't light a torch underwater—but Bacca felt around until he found the trap door that Bill had told him about. Bacca forced it open. The water rushed through. Bacca found himself being carried away on the current. He resisted at first, but eventually let himself go with the flow.

Bacca wooshed through the trap door and down a series of tubes. It was like being inside a giant water slide. (Bacca had, of course, built many of these in his time.) He was twisted all around by the water, until he could no longer tell which way was up. It was very disorienting!

Finally, the tube launched Bacca onto a subterranean drainage grate. He rolled away from the stream of flowing water, stood up, and shook himself like a dog. Bacca's fur was naturally waterproof, but his three-piece suit was going to be wet for hours . . . how annoying!

Where was he now? Bacca surveyed the scene around him. Beside the grate where the water drained off, Bacca saw a large clearing with a floor of stone blocks. To one side was an arch made of andesite. Into the top of it were etched the words: "DUNGEON MAZE." Set into the wall next to it was a familiar looking block of mycelium with writing on it.

"Oh great," Bacca said. "Here we go again."

Yet even as he smoothed his wrinkled, wet suit, he reminded himself that there were things far worse than being a bit wet.

Bacca lit a torch and peered at the new riddle before him. The stone read:

The dungeon maze has many inhabitants.
But only one is the emerald hare.
The hare is the key to solving the maze.
(Or maybe it's vice versa.)

Bacca looked away from the riddle and stared blankly into the entrance of the dungeon maze.

"How can it be *both* a maze and a dungeon?" he said to nobody in particular. "Maybe one man's maze is another man's . . . dungeon?" He shook his head in confusion. "I dunno. Whatever."

Bacca entered the maze. The walls were red brick and several feet taller than Bacca. The ground beneath him was, improbably, grassy—despite the almost total and complete lack of natural sunlight.

Generally, Bacca liked mazes. He had built his share of them, usually to amuse his friends. He was always sure to give them plenty of twists, turns, and surprises. You could tell a lot about a crafter based on what they put in their mazes. Bacca wondered if the creepers in The Creep had built this one. If so, he wondered what it would tell him about them.

As Bacca left the drainage grate behind, he thought that for just a moment, he could hear a noise like a very faint whispering on the wind.

He paused and sniffed the air. It smelled like many strange things, with just a hint of . . . creeper! It probably meant he was getting closer to the creepers' lair, or wherever they were keeping the Dragon Orb.

Excited and encouraged, he headed deeper into the strange, dark maze.

There was quite a kerfuffle among the creepers. They had hardly been able to contain themselves. Quite a few had worked hard to silence the others. When Bacca finally entered the dungeon maze and passed out of view, they finally allowed themselves to speak.

"I think he heard us!" one of creepers said in evident alarm.

"I'm not surprised," said another. "You were practically screaming."

"I was excited," the first creeper said defensively. "He got to see Bill! *Nobody* gets to see Bill! And he was an iron golem. Who knew?"

"I thought you said *you'd* seen him," said the second creeper.

"I did . . ." said the first creeper. "I . . . uhm . . . just forgot."

The creepers next turned their collective attention to Bacca's new task.

"How's he going to fare in the dungeon maze?" one of them wondered. "After all, the emerald hare is an entirely different beast. It's not like Bill at all!"

The creepers nodded in agreement on this point.

"I think we made the riddle too easy for this one," a creeper added. "'The hare is the key'? It's so obvious. He's going to figure it out right away."

"Are you kidding?" said another. "I think we made it too *hard*. This one's a real head-scratcher. After all, you can't just build a mirror and see the emerald hare. Or wait . . . *can* you?"

"What about the Wizard?" said another. "He still lives in the maze. He might know a thing or two."

"Shhh," said another creeper. "Don't tell him about the Wizard!"

"Bacca's not going to hear us *now*, is he?" the prior creeper shot back defensively.

The creepers looked toward the entrance of the dungeon maze. It seemed to all the creepers that they were increasingly unsure of what Bacca would or wouldn't be able to do. Their world was changing. By inviting a master crafter like Bacca to their server, they had taken an enormous risk that could potentially upset everything. All of them knew it.

Now all they could do was watch Bacca and wait to see what happened next. . . .

Chapter Seven

As he made his way down the twisting corridors of the dungeon maze, Bacca wondered what it would take to catch an emerald rabbit. Did it eat emerald carrots? Bacca calculated the steps it would take to dig up some emeralds and craft them into a carrot shape. It actually wouldn't be all that difficult, he decided. Not for an experienced crafter like himself. He expected, however, that solving this riddle would not be that easy. These creepers were not to be trusted with obvious answers.

Bacca arrived at the first junction in the maze having seen no green rabbits to speak of. Both branching hallways looked identical. But while one was silent, the other held the distinct sound of people. More specifically, people chatting. The conversation sounded friendly. Intrigued, Bacca turned down the hallway containing the voices.

The tunnel took several twists and turns, and the voices became louder with each one. After a few moments, Bacca rounded a corner and their source became clear. It was three villagers—a farmer, a librarian, and a blacksmith. Bacca was confused, but not unhappy to see them. He just thought it was strange that they'd wandered all the way down here.

"Hello!" Bacca said, trying to sound friendly. "Are you villagers lost?"

They looked him up and down.

"Why, no," said the farmer. "Are you?"

Touché, thought Bacca, realizing it probably seemed just as odd to the villagers to stumble upon him.

"I'm here trying to help some dragons find an orb," Bacca said. "It's, uh, complicated."

"I see," said the farmer. "We're villagers. We live here."

Bacca couldn't believe what he was hearing.

"What, in the dungeon maze?" Bacca said.

"Sure," said the farmer. "There are a bunch of us in here. It has everything we need. There's even a village."

"But isn't it confusing to live in a maze?" Bacca said.

The villagers shook their heads.

"If you know where it goes, it's not a maze, is it?" quipped the librarian. "And we know all the ways around it."

"Yes," said the blacksmith. "It has the advantage of only confusing outsiders, like, um . . . well, like you."

"But how do you even exist in a maze?" Bacca said, turning to the farmer. "What do you farm down here?"

"Why, I farm the moss that grows on the rocks," the farmer said. "It's delicious. Fry it up with some butter and a little salt and pepper? There's nothing better."

Bacca was skeptical. He would stick to raw fish, thank you very much.

"Well anyhow, I'm trying to solve a riddle that says I have to find an emerald hare . . . which is like a rabbit, I guess," Bacca said. "Does that sound familiar to any of you?"

The villagers looked at one another.

"Emerald hare, eh?" said the farmer. "I've heard of stranger things. Not much stranger, granted. But maybe one or two stranger things."

"Are you sure it wasn't emerald hair, H-A-I-R?" asked the librarian. "I could never pull that off with my color scheme, of course. Maybe if I lived in a green forest instead of a dungeon maze . . ."

"A rabbit might turn green if it was dead for a while," added the blacksmith. "Is this emerald hare you're looking for definitely alive?"

"I think so," Bacca said. "But the riddle wasn't very specific."

The villagers thought about what to do.

"Why don't you come with us to town?" suggested the farmer. "Someone there might know."

"Where is 'town'?" Bacca asked.

"Why, in the middle of the maze, of course," the farmer said. "Just follow us."

The villagers turned and began to stride down the twisting corridors. Whenever a junction presented itself, they confidently turned either left or right. It was clear they knew this place like the backs of their hands. They made so many turns that soon Bacca lost track. He realized with mounting anxiety that he would not be able to find his way back to the entrance without help. But that meant there was only one thing he could do, which was to confidentally keep pushing forward, deeper into the maze, in search of the emerald hare.

Now and then, they encountered other villagers headed the opposite direction. They greeted one another on friendly terms, but the travelling villagers usually cast Bacca a suspicious eye. Bacca wondered if it was because of his hairy face, his wet, wrinkled suit, or something else entirely. Maybe they just didn't like strangers.

Just when Bacca thought the maze couldn't possibly keep going, the villagers took one final turn and the pathway opened into a large clearing with many different maze corridors leading away from it. Inside this clearing were houses and shops and buildings of all types. The place was brightly lit by torches and also stones in the ceiling that naturally radiated yellow light. There were even pens filled with animals. And, of course, villagers. Lots and lots of villagers.

Bacca was quite surprised.

"I've seen villages crop up in some strange places," he said. "But this one takes the cake."

The farmer pointed over at the animal pens.

"You might start there," the farmer said. "A few people here raise rabbits for rabbit stew. Maybe some of them are green?"

Bacca thanked the farmer and made his way across the village and over to the animal pens. He looked high and low for green rabbits, but saw only the usual black and white ones. The rabbits in their pens were skittish and hopped away when Bacca drew near. A few passing villagers thought he might be a rabbit thief stalking his prey. Bacca assured them his intentions were honorable.

"Maybe I could dye a rabbit green," Bacca thought out loud. "If I liquefied an emerald somehow, and then . . ."

"Dye a rabbit?" said a high-pitched voice. "Why on earth would you do that? Did the rabbit *ask* to be dyed?"

It was one of the villager children. A young boy with bright yellow hair. He had wandered over from a nearby farm. He looked up at Bacca curiously.

"I need an emerald hare," Bacca explained. "You don't know of any green rabbits who live in this maze, do you?"

The young boy scratched his head.

"No," said the boy. "*I* don't."

Bacca wondered what that emphasis on "I" meant.

"So, *somebody* knows?" Bacca asked.

"The Wizard might," the boy said.

Suddenly, as if carried on the breeze, Bacca thought he heard the sound of a hundred very tiny voices shrieking in unison. He decided it must have been his imagination.

"Sorry," Bacca said. "What were you saying about a wizard?"

"*The* Wizard," the boy said. "And he knows lots of things. Whenever we have a question, there's a good chance the Wizard knows the answer. He's been down here for ages. Seen all kinds of stuff in his day."

"Why do you call him the Wizard?" Bacca asked.

"He knows how to make things," the boy said. "It's kind of hard to describe."

"Hmm," said Bacca, thinking that of all his options, going to see the Wizard was a pretty good one. "Can you take me to him?"

Just then a voice rang out from across the rabbit pens.

"Come to dinner! Your rabbit stew's getting cold!"

"That's my mom," said the boy. "I gotta go. But here . . . I can tell you how to find the Wizard."

Bacca listened as the boy with the yellow hair described a series of twists and turns leading away from the village and back into the maze. Bacca nodded dumbly and tried to memorize all of them as best as he could. He had the feeling that these villagers were used to complicated trips.

Bacca thanked him, and the boy ran off to dinner. Bacca made for a tunnel leading back into the maze.

Once inside, Bacca followed the boy's directions carefully. When the directions said make a left, Bacca made a left. When they said to take the fork to the right, Bacca took the fork to the right. It was very challenging because of the sheer number of turns. On top of this, many of the maze's corridors looked identical. There were almost no defining characteristics. Bacca wondered how in the world these villagers managed it. He supposed it took a lifetime of practice.

More quickly than seemed possible, Bacca had exhausted all of the boy's directions—he'd followed all them perfectly, he was sure—but as he looked around, he didn't see anything that looked like a destination. He certainly didn't see a wizard. Bacca stood at a dead end. He faced only a brick wall.

This couldn't be right, could it?

Bacca crept forward and knocked on the wall with his fist. It did not give. Then he ran his hands along the walls looking for openings or levers or trap doors, but he didn't find anything in the way of a secret opening to a wizard's lair. Or, really, anything at all.

Bacca leaned against the wall, frustrated, and wondered if he could even remember how to get back to the village.

"Are you lost?" a disembodied voice said.

It was a gentle voice, and also high-pitched . . . as if it came from someone very small.

"Hello?" Bacca said. He looked around but saw nobody. His heart sank as he imagined dealing with another hermit like Bill.

"I'm up here, silly," the voice said.

Bacca looked.

High above his head, a purple bat hovered near the ceiling.

"Can I help you?" it asked.

"I'm looking for a wizard," Bacca said. "Or maybe it's 'the Wizard.' A boy gave me directions to where I could find him. But I'm worried that maybe I went to the wrong place."

"It happens," said the Bat. "We all get lost now and then. Lucky for you, I'm here."

"How is that lucky?" Bacca asked.

"Well, for one, I'm the Wizard," the bat said. "For another, I decided to take pity on you and say hello . . . instead of letting you just bounce around this maze like all of the other people who go looking for me but never think to look up."

Bacca suddenly had a lot of questions.

"I suddenly have a lot of questions," Bacca told the Wizard.

"That's fine," the Wizard said. "Let's go to my workshop. I'll answer them there."

And with that, the purple bat began to flap its way back down the corridor.

Bacca saw no alternative but to follow. The bat flew quickly. Bacca ran in order to keep up with it.

They raced down the corridors of the maze, sometimes passing bewildered villagers, and taking the turns with so much speed that Bacca seriously doubted he would ever remember the way they'd come.

"If this bat is getting me confused on purpose, it's going to be in big trouble," Bacca said to himself.

Eventually, the bat took a turn down an old, dusty corner of the maze. Here, the grass was completely undisturbed. Bacca's feet left big indentations as he walked.

"Don't worry about that," the bat said brightly. "I don't get many guests in my workshop. Don't worry, we're almost there."

Bacca followed the bat around a corner, and the way before them suddenly opened into a giant room filled with crafting materials. There were ingots and stones and blocks of every size and color. One pool in the floor supplied an endless stream of fresh water. Another supplied fresh lava. Different objects—some complete, some only half crafted—were stacked in the corners, sometimes in precarious, teetering piles that stretched nearly to the ceiling.

The bat perched atop a pile of iron ingots that was roughly the same height as Bacca.

"Sorry about the clutter," it said halfheartedly. "I'm always busy crafting something—or trying to— and the projects have a way of getting away from me. I suppose that's why you're here, eh? You want something crafted?"

Bacca opened his mouth to say "not exactly," but the bat just kept talking.

"That's why they call me 'the Wizard.' Because I can craft things. Here, that's as rare as wizardry. This is such a strange server plane. We've got twenty different kinds of dragons, and creepers who behave like organized criminals, but there's virtually no one here who can craft. Other servers are full of crafters. I've heard all the stories. In those places, anybody and everybody can make things. They're all builders. Great crafters! Creative crafters! Crafters limited only by their imaginations! Why, there's a long list. There's . . ."

Here, the Wizard named a string of famous, talented crafters, many of whom Bacca knew well. The list ended with ". . . and then there's Bacca, the most famous of all."

Bacca let out a little laugh. (He tried to hold it in, so it sounded more like a snort.)

"Are you okay?" the Wizard asked.

"Yeah," Bacca said. "It's just funny."

"What's funny?"

"Well . . . I'm Bacca," said Bacca.

"You?" said the Wizard, quite bewildered. "Really? Really and truly? You're *the* Bacca? As in *Bacca*-Bacca?"

"Sure," Bacca said. "I can prove it too. What are you working on right now?"

The Wizard looked at him doubtfully, but couldn't resist.

"I've been working on making a jukebox," the bat said, and flew over to where a pile of wooden planks was stacked next to a large diamond. "It's been giving me a bit of trouble, to tell you the truth."

"Let me see," Bacca said, bending down to examine the Wizard's work.

The Wizard hovered in midair and watched carefully as Bacca began to assemble the different components. Bacca worked swiftly, as if he already knew exactly where each piece should go. Just a few short moments later, a finished jukebox sat before them.

"There you go," Bacca said. "All done. Your problem was you were trying to use nine wooden planks. You really only need eight."

"So that's why I couldn't get it to fit!" the Wizard said.

"What else have you got?" Bacca asked.

"One of the villagers did ask me to craft him a new piston," the Wizard replied cagily, as if this were not a very complicated item at all.

"No problem!" Bacca replied.

Bacca began to sift through the workshop's plentiful piles of material. Soon he had assembled three wooden planks, four cobblestones, an iron ingot, and a glistening redstone. He stacked them together on the floor, and began using the Wizard's tools to create a perfectly-functioning piston. When it was done, Bacca tested it by using it to push a few blocks around the workshop.

"There you go," Bacca said, handing it over to the Wizard. "It works great."

The Wizard had to agree that it did.

"Maybe you *are* Bacca," the Wizard said. "But one final test. Craft me a . . . a . . . sticky diamond minecart."

Bacca smiled but did not move.

"What?" the Wizard said slyly. "Can't do it? I thought you were a famous crafter."

"There's no such thing as a sticky diamond minecart!" Bacca replied.

The Wizard fluttered about excitedly.

"Wow!" the little bat said. "That's right. You really are Bacca."

"I'm glad you're finally convinced," Bacca said.

"But now I'm confused," the Wizard said, hovering close. "If you're Bacca, then what in the wide world of Minecraft do you need with me?"

Bacca told the story of how he had been visited in his server by the Diamond Dragon, and about his quest to retrieve the Dragon Orb.

"This latest riddle seems to say that I have to catch an emerald rabbit that lives somewhere in this maze," Bacca concluded. "I've found some nice villagers who live in the middle of the maze, but no rabbit so far. Some of the villagers thought you might know where I could find it."

The Wizard stopped hovering and set itself back down atop a half-built minecart hopper.

"So . . . any idea where I can find a green-colored bunny?" Bacca asked.

"As a matter of fact, I do," said the bat. "It's just, um, a little complicated."

Bacca wondered how complicated it could be to catch a rabbit. They didn't seem like very smart animals. And they were known to do almost anything for a carrot.

"You'll have to trust me," the bat continued. "See, there's a witch who lives in this maze. Not a 'witch' in the way I'm a 'wizard,' but a real, proper witch, with a pointy hat and a wart on her nose and a big sack full of unpleasant potions she throws at people she doesn't like—which is everybody. She's always attacking people for no reason. Everybody hates her. What I need you to do is kill the witch—or at least convince her to leave the maze. Then I can show you where the emerald hare is."

"Wait . . . if you know where it is, why can't you just show me now?" Bacca asked.

"Hang on, I'm not done yet!" the Wizard said. "I said it was complicated. I also need you to make a map. To the witch's lair. People have been looking for it for years, but we've never found it. I need you to make a map of everywhere you go in the maze. Circle on the map where the witch lives. Then bring the map back to me. That way, we can go to her lair and verify that you've done what I asked."

"This is a very strange errand," Bacca said. "Are you absolutely sure you can't just tell me where the rabbit is? What if I show you how to do some crafting as a trade-off?"

"No, sorry," said the little bat. "Take care of the witch. Make me a map of how you got there. Only then will I show you how to find the emerald hare."

"Okay," Bacca said with a sigh, "but this feels *over*complicated."

"Here," the Wizard said, flying over to a desk cluttered with different odds and ends. "There's a scroll of paper and a pen and ink in this desk. You can use them to draw the map as you go."

"Thanks . . . I think," Bacca said, adding the supplies to his inventory.

"Perfect," said the Wizard. "Off you go. Come back when the witch is gone. And make sure to make a detailed map!"

"Yeah, yeah," Bacca said. "I got it."

Bacca left the Wizard's workshop and stepped back out into the maze. He breathed a deep sigh. If there was one thing Bacca hated, it was busywork. And he had the distinct feeling that the little bat was making things more difficult than they needed to be.

Still, Bacca had faced down many witches in his day. If he had to face one more to solve this riddle, then he was happy to do it. Making maps was not one of his regular activities, but sometimes it could be fun to try something new. Bacca always tried to look on the bright side.

He set off down the corridor, tracing his route in miniature on the paper the Wizard had given him. Every so often, he looked up from his page to check for witches. He rounded a bend in the corridor, and soon the Wizard's workshop passed entirely out of sight.

"This is very strange," one creeper said to another.

They were clustered together in the shadows at the edge of the dungeon maze. One of their group, a spy, had just returned—out of breath and panting—to relate what he had overheard in the Wizard's workshop.

"Very strange indeed," a different creeper agreed. "The Wizard knows exactly what Bacca needs to do. He could have told him how to solve our riddle then and there."

"Don't you see?" said another creeper. "The Wizard is using Bacca to get revenge on the witch. He wants to break the spell."

"I still think it's a good riddle," another creeper said defensively. "It's just taken a slightly different turn than we expected. That's all."

"I wonder what Bacca's going to do next?" one of the creepers said, scowling at the creeper-spy who had only just got his breath back. "Well . . . ? That's your cue. Get back in there and get us some more information!!!"

The creeper-spy sped back into the dungeon maze, keeping to the shadows, hot on Bacca's trail.

Someone had once told Bacca that the way to beat a maze was to keep making lefts at every turn. That way, you'd eventually arrive at the outer walls of the maze, and you'd be able to work it out from there. The problem with that approach, Bacca also knew, was that sometimes there were places within a maze that were just big square blocks. If you hit one of them, you'd just keep turning left and going in a square forever!

Because of this, Bacca now and then also took a right.

He explored the corridors of the dungeon maze for what felt like hours. Now and then he encountered an interesting feature. A fountain made of sandstone blocks shaped like an enormous fish (but sadly, bereft of any real fish) was one of his favorites. There was also a two-headed gargoyle that seemed to have been crafted out of giant blocks of yellow sponge. (Bacca hoped it might be alive—and tried talking to it—but if the gargoyle could understand him, it didn't let on.)

He also encountered several groups of villagers making their ways to different places. They were all cautious but friendly. Bacca made a point to ask if they knew anything about the witch. Mostly they didn't.

One villager said: "Witches, sure. They live up on the Overworld. You'd have to leave the fortress to find them though. I wouldn't want to do that."

"No," Bacca clarified. "I'm looking for a witch who lives *here*, inside of the dungeon maze."

"Inside the maze?" the villager responded, dumbfounded. "Well that would be just awful. I hope there's not a witch down here."

Bacca did not press the point.

He hated to admit it, but the mapmaking was turning out to be a sensible idea. The maze was enormous. If he had not chosen to make recordings of each place he'd already been, the chances of getting lost and going over the same places again and again would have been very great indeed. Then again, Bacca thought to himself, he wouldn't be making a map in the first place if the Wizard had just *told him where to find the emerald hare.*

It was safe to say that Bacca was having mixed feelings about this new adventure.

At one point, Bacca's journey through the maze took him back to the village at its center. Bacca saw a familiar face lounging in one of the stables. It was the boy with the yellow hair.

"How was your rabbit stew?" Bacca asked him.

"Good," the boy said. "It was cold, but I like cold rabbit stew."

"I like fish when it's cold," Bacca said. "Uncooked actually. Maybe we have something in common."

The boy nodded in agreement.

"Did you find the Wizard?" the boy asked.

"Yes," Bacca said. "He told me to find a witch and get rid of her. And I have to make a map of my travels to find her. But nobody I've talked to knows anything about a witch."

"My grandfather used to talk about a witch, but that was many years ago," said the boy. "I don't remember any details. Sorry. I wish I could tell you more."

"That's okay," said Bacca. "It's more than anybody else has been able to tell me."

"Oh, well good then," said the boy happily.

"I thought this mapmaking was going to be a stupid waste of my time," Bacca added. "But it's actually been really helpful in keeping me from getting lost. I'm glad the Wizard suggested it. Or, required it, I guess."

"Yeah," the boy said, nodding. "That's the thing about the Wizard. When he gives you a task, there's usually a good reason behind it."

Bacca said farewell to the boy with the yellow hair, and spent a few more minutes questioning other villagers. A few thought they had "maybe" heard about a witch in the maze a long time ago, but nobody knew where she lived now. Bacca tried not to get discouraged. When he decided there was nothing else to be learned from the villagers, he set off again into the twists and turns of the maze.

It was easy to lose track of time. Bacca was soon sure that he had walked for hours and hours, or maybe even for days and days. He walked and walked and walked. Then he walked some more. His drawings of the maze became long and detailed. He was hungry. There were no raw fish to be seen. There were also no witches.

The one development that felt like progress was finding the outer wall of the maze. Bacca was reasonably sure he'd been able to find the edge. This allowed him to understand the outermost borders of the maze, and how much he had left to explore.

After what seemed like a truly epic period of exploration, Bacca turned down a corridor that felt somehow familiar. A few paces later, Bacca realized why.

"Oh no," he said to himself. "I'm back to the Wizard's workshop. And I didn't find the witch at all!"

Bacca went through a range of emotions. At least one of them was the emotion that makes you want to grab a little loudmouthed bat by the toe and start squeezing until it told you where to find an emerald hare. Bacca tried to fight this emotion—at least for the moment—as he barged back into the workshop.

The Wizard was fixing a minecart with a broken wheel. He held a tiny hammer in his wing and an itty-bitty chisel in the other. He put both down when he saw Bacca.

"You didn't find the witch," the Wizard said, flying over.

It was a statement, not a question.

"No," Bacca said, feeling annoyed. "I sure didn't."

"On the upside," said the little bat. "You found the emerald hare."

"No I didn't," Bacca said. "What're you talking about?"

The bat smiled, baring a set of tiny, sharp teeth. Bacca had a feeling as though someone were playing a practical joke on him. A joke he didn't get. Bacca looked around, ready for somebody to start laughing at him.

"Take out the map you drew and show it to me," the Wizard said.

"But it's pages and pages," replied Bacca.

"Then lay out the pages together on the ground to form one big map," the Wizard said.

"Okaaaay," said Bacca. He was skeptical, but did as he was told.

Bacca carefully took the pages on which he'd drawn the maze's winding corridors and arranged them together on the floor of the workshop. As he did so, the tiny bat hovered near his shoulder, looking on and smiling approvingly. When Bacca finished, he looked up at the bat.

"There you go," Bacca said. "That's everything."

"Now take a few steps back from it," said the Wizard.

Bacca thought this was silly, but obliged.

"Now take a look at the entire thing—all of it together," said the bat. "What do you see?"

It slowly dawned on Bacca. The maze had a body, four little jutting side-tunnels like legs, a large portion above the body like a head . . . and two long extensions that suddenly looked a whole lot like long floppy ears.

"The maze looks like a rabbit!" Bacca cried.

"And what color is the floor of the maze?" the Wizard asked.

Bacca recalled that while the walls were blocks of red brick, the ground underfoot was always fresh grass. Fresh *green* grass.

"Oh my goodness," Bacca said. "The emerald hare *is* the maze."

"Exactly," the Wizard said. It stopped to perch on Bacca's shoulder the way a parrot might sit on a pirate it was especially familiar with.

"But . . ." Bacca stammered. "What am I supposed to do now? Have I solved the riddle? This is still confusing."

"Take a look again," the Wizard said. "Is the rabbit a perfect rabbit?"

"Well, my map-drawing penmanship isn't perfect," Bacca began. "But it does appear that there's a chunk missing from one of the rabbit's ears. It looks like a chocolate bunny that somebody took a bite out of."

"Right," said the Wizard. "So what does that tell you?"

"Maybe I missed something?" Bacca wondered.

The Wizard nodded.

"That's where the witch lives," the tiny bat said. "The entrance to her lair is secret, but you can find it if you know it's there. Once you go inside, you'll have walked the entire length of the emerald hare.

I think that then, and only then, you'll have solved the riddle."

"Wow," Bacca said. "Thanks." He couldn't shake the feeling that the Wizard could have somehow made all of this a whole lot easier. But he was too excited to dwell on it. He was making progress. Now it was time to solve the riddle!

"You're welcome," said the Wizard, taking off back into the air.

Bacca's hands were far too large for him to properly shake hands with the tiny bat, but he extended a hairy finger and the bat was able to shake it.

"You were certainly secretive about the maze," Bacca said. "Before I go, is there anything you're not telling me about the witch?"

The bat rubbed its chin.

"Probably not," it eventually determined.

"'Probably not'?" Bacca said.

"Yes," the bat said. "That's right."

Then the Wizard gave him a little wink.

Bacca gathered up his map and headed off to find the lair of the witch.

chapter eight

Bacca ran his hands across the brick walls, looking for anything that might be the opening to a secret passage to where a witch lived. According to his map, he was standing right on the "ear" of the rabbit where the witch should be. There had to be a way to access the missing area. Bacca felt all along the wall, then knocked on it gently with one of his pickaxes. Bacca knew it would be very possible to break the wall down or simply tunnel under it, but something about that felt dangerous. Bacca had dealt with witches a few times before; there were usually consequences for just barging in.

Then Bacca's foot caught on something in the floor of the passageway. Bacca took a knee and began to examine the spot more closely. He used his hands to clear away the grass and soil. He realized he had found a trap door.

"Now we're talking!" Bacca said.

He carefully opened the door and peered inside. It was dark, but Bacca lit a torch and hopped in. He found himself in another hallway, much smaller than the halls of the maze. Immediately the smell hit him. Witches.

Witches themselves did not have a smell, of course. Or, if they did, it was entirely lost underneath the smell of the twenty or so different kinds of fragrant potions that they always seemed to be cooking at any given time. It was an odd combination of fire, boiling water, and lots and lots of ingredients. Once you smelled it, you never forgot it. If you got too close, the stench would stick to your clothes for days. (Bacca's suit was still moist from diving into the pool. Now it was going to smell like witch on top of that. "Great," he muttered sarcastically. "My dry cleaning bill is going to be through the roof this month!")

Bacca walked down the corridor in the direction of the mixture of strange smells. Soon he also heard bubbling sounds—a sure sign that he was getting closer to a witch. Then he saw a set of stairs and a hatch in the ceiling. He knew what he had to do.

The best way to take on a witch was to rush in quickly and give it several swift whacks. Otherwise, they could hit you with potions and you might be in trouble. With this in mind, Bacca took Betty out of his inventory and made a few practice chops against the wall. Then he steadied his nerves and threw open the trap door above.

Jumping through, Bacca saw that he was indeed inside a witch's laboratory. All manner of large black cauldrons burbled in the cavernous room around him. Glass tubes connected by copper piping synthesized different heated liquids. There were tables with large stacks of exotic ingredients piled high atop them. Bacca saw all of this in a flash. Then, suddenly, there was a splashing sound. Bacca realized he was now suffering one of the disadvantages of leaping before he looked.

Bacca had landed right in the middle of a cauldron. The strange smell of its contents bubbled up over him. It was really unpleasant.

"Yuck," Bacca said, crawling out of the cauldron and knocking over a brewing stand beside it. "So much for an inconspicuous entrance."

No sooner were these words out of Bacca's mouth than they were proved true.

From the back of the lair, a dark and mysterious figure emerged. It was a witch, and a large one at that! She towered over Bacca and stared down at him angrily. She had a long nose with a bright red wart on it, and a tall hat with a brass buckle that was turning green. She had hairy eyebrows and thin lips. She looked at Bacca like he was a bug she wanted to squash.

"Who are you?" she cackled. "I suppose you want to get rid of me, eh?"

"If getting rid of you will solve the riddle, then that's what I'm here to do," Bacca said. He used his glistening diamond axe to pick his fangs. He hoped it looked intimidating, but then again, he was also wet and smelly from having just crawled out of her cauldron . . .

The witch smiled as though this was cute.

"Oh, I've heard about *you*," the witch said. "Word travels fast down here. Bacca the famous crafter. Bacca with his legions of fans. Bacca *this* and Bacca *that*. Well I've got news for you! Now you're in *my* lair, and I'm the one in charge. Get it?"

Bacca sighed. Why did bullies always have "news for you"?

"Listen, we can still do this peacefully," Bacca said. "I'm sure you've had a good run here. But maybe now it's time for you to move on somewhere else. Wouldn't it be nice to relocate, find some other witches, and settle down as a nice little horde? Or, wait, would that be a coven? You know, I can never remember the correct terminology . . ."

"I'm not sure you fully understand your predicament," said the witch confidently, reaching for her satchel. Witches were quick on the draw with their potions, just like old west cowboys with their guns. Plus, you never knew exactly what the potions were going to do. But it was usually something bad.

Now that he had ruined the chance for his favorite witch-attacking technique—charging in before they had a chance to draw—Bacca prepared for his second-favorite technique: dodging a whole bunch of potions while you tried to get close enough to strike back.

The witch's hand hovered over her potion inventory.

"That's a nice axe you have there," the witch said, taunting Bacca. "Of course to hit me with it, you'd have to see me . . ."

Then the witch did something Bacca was not expecting. She reached into her satchel and pulled out a clear potion . . . and drank it. An instant later, she vanished into the air.

Bacca had only a moment to react. Trying to hit an invisible witch while she threw potion after potion at you—probably while she was circle strafing—was not Bacca's idea of a good time. He might be able to pull it off, sure, but he also might end up witch-food. In the split-second Bacca had to react, he decided on another, better approach . . .

Potion war!

The witch was at a disadvantage because Bacca had surprised her in her workshop. There were still tables piled high with ingredients that anyone could use to make potions. Perhaps the witch did not know that in addition to being a master crafter, Bacca was also a master at brewing potions. But if that was the case . . . she was about to find out.

Instead of charging the invisible witch, Bacca leapt to the side where a table of ingredients and an empty cauldron were waiting. Instants later, a potion of harming materialized out of thin air across the room and careened into the spot where Bacca had been standing. The vile black liquid exploded against the stone floor with an evil *hissssss*.

Yikes, Bacca thought. This witch was not messing around.

With blazing speed, Bacca began to rummage for all the ingredients he needed for a potion of his own. He took nether wart, a golden carrot, and a fermented spider eye and mixed them together in a cauldron. Another potion of harming materialized out of thin air and sailed past him. Bacca carefully ducked out of the way. The cauldron's effects on the ingredients were practically instant, and moments later Bacca was drinking down his own concoction.

He held his hairy arm in front of his face, and found that he could not see it. The plan had worked. He had made his own potion of invisibility! Now it was a fair fight. At least for the moment . . .

"Not so much fun when somebody turns the tables on you, is it?" Bacca said with a laugh.

"Argh!" the witch cried out in frustration. "I'm still going to get you!"

Another potion of harming materialized and flew across the room. But this time, it shattered nowhere near Bacca. The witch was firing blind.

Bacca considered his next move. If he made his own potions of harming—which, being a master at brewing potions, he could easily do—then he and the witch would just be invisible people throwing potions at targets they could not see. It would take *all day* to fight that way, thought Bacca. And he was in a hurry to get the dragons back their orb. There had to be a better way, so he hatched a different plan.

While the angry witch continued to "spray and pray" by throwing potions of harming everywhere, Bacca charged over to a different cauldron. Into this one he combined a golden carrot with a redstone and some nether wart. When it was brewed and in the bottle, he did not immediately drink it. Instead, he silently crept to the wall where a trio of torches provided the room's sole illumination. Now and then, the witch threw another potion (and uttered an old-timey-sounding witch-curse), but the potions all missed.

Bacca grabbed a water bottle from the nearest pile of brewing ingredients, and used the water to extinguish the torches. The room was plunged into utter darkness. He heard the witch shriek in surprise. Bacca quickly drank the new potion he had brewed. It was, of course, a potion of night vision. Once again, the room was visible to him—a strange shade of grey, but visible.

Bacca turned his attention to the direction from where the last potion had been thrown. The surprised witch was stumbling around, probably looking for a potion of night vision of her own. Did the rest of her inventory contain only offensive potions? If so, then Bacca was definitely in luck.

Soon Bacca saw what he was waiting for. The witch stumbled in the darkness and knocked into a table of ingredients, sending it toppling over. Bacca sprang into action. He leapt to the spot just where he knew the witch would be. He felt himself connect with the witch and sent her reeling back. Then he took Betty out of his inventory and prepared to strike.

"Okay, you win!" cried the witch.

At that very moment, her potion wore off and she became visible to Bacca again.

"If you let me go, then I'll leave and never come back," the witch said. "I'll knock down the wall I put up to separate my lair from the rest of the maze. And I'll even let the Wizard out from under my curse."

Bacca paused.

"Wait . . . there's a curse on the Wizard?" Bacca asked.

"Sure there is," the witch said.

"What *kind* of curse?" Bacca asked.

"For starters, he wasn't always a bat," the witch said. "He used to be a villager. On top of that, he used to be able to come and go as he pleased. But I placed an enchantment on him so he can never leave this maze."

"That was certainly lousy of you," Bacca said disapprovingly. "What made you do something so mean?"

"He was . . ." the witch had difficulty speaking, as though there was something she could not bear to admit.

"Out with it!" Bacca ordered.

"Fine," said the witch. "He was better at crafting than me! *And* better at brewing potions, if you can believe it. Me, a witch! I'm supposed to be the best. I got so jealous! He was always showing me up whenever there was some kind of crafting competition. I got tired of coming in second place. So when I learned how to put curses on people, he was my first and only target."

"Well, now we are going to set some things right," Bacca said sternly. "And you are going to help. If you obey me, I just *might* let you go."

"Oh, thank you," said the witch.

"Don't thank me yet," said Bacca. "First things first. I want you to hand over that satchel of potions you're carrying."

The witch frowned sadly but hoisted her bag of potions into the air. Bacca took it from her. Then he took each of the potions and dumped them down a drain.

"They were my finest creations," wept the witch.

"And you used them to be a jerk," Bacca said. "Now, get back on your feet. You can swing a pickaxe, can't you? Well, get out a pickaxe and help me connect your secret lair back with the rest of the maze."

Bacca relit the torches just as his own potions wore off. The witch looked grumpy, but she was true to her word. Working together, they hacked away at the blocks that formed the walls to the witch's home. Sparks flew as their pickaxes chiseled away. Great mounds of dust and debris began to gather at their feet.

"This is hot work," the witch said. "I'd sure like a drink."

"You can have a drink," Bacca said. Then he added: "*Of water.*"

Bacca watched carefully as the witch took a glass bottle full of water and drained it. He wanted to make sure she didn't drink a potion. Witches were not known for their honesty. Or, really, for anything other than throwing nasty potions and being generally unpleasant.

"Okay," Bacca said. "Break's over. Let's get back to work."

Working together, they continued to smash down the walls that hid the witch's lair from the rest of the maze. Eventually, they broke through the outer wall entirely. Bacca stopped to compare their efforts to his map.

"Yes!" said Bacca. "We've done it. Now if we build it up and make it look like the rest of the maze, the rabbit will have its ear back. The emerald hare will be complete!"

Bacca put up brick walls around where the witch's lair had been, and replaced her stone floors with blocks of green grass. Bacca overturned and destroyed all of the witch's brewing equipment so it could never again be used to make dangerous potions. Before long, it was as though the lair had never existed.

"Boo hoo," the witch sniffled. "All my stuff is gone."

"You can go find a new place to make a lair . . . far away from where you can hurt anyone," Bacca suggested. "But first you have to take the curse off of the Wizard. And apologize. I want you to apologize, too."

"Uh oh," said the witch nervously. "Witches aren't very good at that."

"Well you'd better *get* good," Bacca said. "And fast."

Bacca grabbed the reluctant witch by the back of her collar and marched her through the maze. Eventually, they arrived back at the Wizard's workshop. A couple of times, Bacca caught the witch looking longingly down one of the forking corridors, as though she was thinking about making a break for it.

"Nuh uh," Bacca said when this happened, and shook his head sternly. "Don't even think about it."

Bacca entered the Wizard's workshop triumphantly. The Wizard was very surprised! When he saw the witch, he flew underneath a bucket and hid.

"Ack, the witch!" the tiny bat-voice said.

"Relax," said Bacca. "I'm here too."

The Wizard lifted the bucket just enough to verify this.

"Don't worry," Bacca said. "I took her whole inventory of potions. She's harmless. More importantly, she has something she wants to say to you. *Isn't that right,* witch?"

"Uh, yes," the witch said. "That's right."

The Wizard crawled out from underneath his bucket.

"Why did you bring her here?" the Wizard asked. "I said to get rid of her."

"I'm going to do that," Bacca said. "But first . . ."

Bacca looked at the witch expectantly.

"I'm sorry for turning you into a bat," the witch said with downcast eyes.

"*And?*" Bacca pressed.

"And for putting a hex on you so you could never leave the maze," the witch continued.

"Good," Bacca said. "Now lift the curses."

The witch grumbled, but did as she was told. She waved her hands in the air and said some magic words. When Bacca looked back over at the Wizard, the little bat was gone and a normal-looking villager stood in its place.

"Omigosh!" the Wizard said—he had the same voice, but not quite as high-pitched. "This is wonderful! Thank you, Bacca."

"You're welcome," Bacca said.

"Now, what are you going to do with her?" the Wizard said.

"She's promised to leave and go someplace where she can't hurt anybody with her potions anymore," Bacca said, turning to the witch. *"Isn't that right?"*

"Yes," the witched said sadly. "Now that you've destroyed my lair, there's no point in staying here. I suppose I'll go somewhere out in the wastes and start all over again."

"Yes," said Bacca. "I think that's a very good idea."

No sooner were these words out of Bacca's mouth when a strange glow began to appear in the hallway outside. It was a yellow light that radiated in such a way that it was clearly magic.

"Are *you* doing that?" Bacca asked the witch.

"No!" she cried from beneath her pointy hat. "I promise I'm not. No way."

Bacca turned to the Wizard.

"Don't look at me," he said. "I don't do real magic. But I have a feeling this might be connected to your solving the riddle."

Bacca crept to the doorway of the Wizard's workshop and took a closer look. The glow was coming from a strange beam of light that led away into the dungeon maze.

"I think you should follow it," the Wizard said. "I bet it takes you out of the maze."

Bacca thought this was an excellent idea.

"Thanks again for your help," Bacca said to the Wizard. "And you, witch . . . you're going to be nicer to people from now on, right?"

"I'll, er, do my best," the witch said.

"I think that's the best you're going to get from her," the Wizard said. "It's a sliding scale with witches, you know."

Bacca decided the Wizard was probably right, but he still gave the witch one final stern glance.

"Will I see you again?" Bacca asked the Wizard.

"Hmm, it's possible," said the Wizard. "Now that I can leave the maze, I think I might be due for a vacation. Maybe I'll go visit my brother in the lands to the west."

"That sounds nice," Bacca said. "Have safe travels."

"The same to you," said the Wizard.

And with that, Bacca headed back into the maze to follow the magic glowing beam of light.

chapter nine

The creeper spy was beyond breathless when he emerged from the maze. In fact, he was panting so hard he was unable to speak for some time. The rest of the creepers crowded around impatiently, waiting for any hint of what the news might be. When the spy was finally able to tell them what had transpired, a great fracas broke out through the creeper ranks.

"We've lost the witch!" cried one creeper. "That was never part of the plan!"

"She was one of our fortress's finest residents," said another with a sniffle. "She'd do anything for you. Give you an arm and a leg if you asked. I mean, they wouldn't be *hers* . . . but still."

"What a tragedy," remarked a third creeper. "Who'm I going to get to make all of my potions of harming?"

There was a moment of silence as the creepers considered this loss to their community.

"This Bacca chap is proving quite a wildcard," one of the senior creepers remarked. "Remember, all of this this is designed to *test* him, not to, not to . . . give him a chance to do whatever he pleases."

"If it makes you feel any better," a more junior creeper said, "his next challenge is Gargantua."

The senior creeper's beady eyes suddenly shone with a light they had not radiated for years. He began to laugh, deeply and evilly. It was a disturbing sound, even for the other creepers.

"Gargantua, eh?" the senior creeper said. From the tone of his voice, it seemed this was very satisfying to him indeed.

"That's right, sir," someone said.

"This will be the most dangerous test yet," said the senior creeper. "I'd like to see what Bacca does with *him*! It's not possible to defeat Gargantua! I don't even know if a dragon could. This hairy little crafter may have had a few lucky breaks up to this point, but, gentlemen, I have a strong feeling that his luck is about to change."

There was more evil laughter. This time from *all* of the creepers.

"Come on," one of them said. "I'm going to go get a front row seat for this one!"

The rest of the creepers agreed this was a good idea, and hurried off to find a good spot to watch the action.

Off in another part of the dungeon maze, Bacca was following the glowing yellow line. It radiated light and made a faint hum whenever Bacca stepped near it. He had no idea where it was taking him, but from his maps it looked as though he was heading for the emerald hare's mouth. (If it had to be one end or the other, Bacca was fine to take this one, thank you very much.)

Bacca reached a point where the glowing line terminated at a dead end. Yet no sooner did Bacca approach it than he heard the sound of stone grinding against stone and the wall in front of him began to move apart. A cave was revealed beyond it, the mouth covered in red sand.

"Yeah, I'm just going to say this is the rabbit's mouth," Bacca said to himself as he stepped through it and left the maze.

The cave beyond was well lit with torches set into sconces along the walls every few feet. The walkway underfoot changed from grass to dark blocks of stone and obsidian. Ahead of him, Bacca thought for a moment that the passage might dead-end or fall away. Then he got closer and saw that it was only the beginning of a staircase. A staircase leading down. *Way* down.

Bacca had built some very long staircases in his day, but had never seen one quite like this. It led down to the depths below the creeper fortress. Torches along the walls still lit the way, but they seemed to stretch endlessly into the dark obsidian depths.

Beside the staircase, next to the first step, a single mycelium block was affixed to the wall.

Bacca took a deep breath and read the words that had been etched across it:

What do men want?
What do women want?
Those answers won't help you here.
But what does Gargantua want?
That is the key to everything.

"Gargantua," Bacca said to himself. "Hmm. That means 'very big,' I think."

Bacca wondered if Gargantua could be a person. Maybe a giant person. But also, Bacca thought, sometimes big people got nicknames like "Tiny." So this could just be that principle working in reverse. Maybe you called someone Gargantua when they were really quite small.

Bacca decided to keep an eye out for something either very big or very small. Something in *an extreme*.

And then, Bacca thought, the riddle says I should find out what it wants. Hmmm.

With nothing more than this in mind, Bacca began to descend the long staircase.

Soon, Bacca was far underground. He did not know how deep he'd gone—it was easy to lose track—but this was very deep. We weren't talking mine-deep or cavern-deep. This was more like center-of-the-Overworld deep.

As Bacca walked down the obsidian steps, the décor around him took a turn for the macabre and scary. He began to see skeleton skulls used along the walls in place of blocks. When he looked closer at the sconces in the walls that held the torches, he saw that they were skeletal hands.

"How long has *that* been going on?" Bacca wondered. He stopped and looked up the staircase behind him. It was skeletal hands for as far as he could see. Creepy.

Continuing along—but more carefully now—he also began to notice bones in the ceiling above him. Bacca knew that he was underground, but this felt *too* low for a cemetery or burying ground. Whoever wanted these bones to be here had brought them intentionally. *All* of this was intentional.

Intentionally spooky, Bacca thought to himself.

He continued down the staircase, and passed more ghastly, scary constructions. But what he did *not* see was anything (or anybody) very big or very small. Bacca hoped that "Gargantua" would not be so small that Bacca would miss him entirely.

Eventually, Bacca saw that—far ahead of him—the sloping staircase did finally end. Where it terminated, a stone archway was set, and beyond that Bacca could see a high-ceilinged room.

"Finally," Bacca said to himself. "I thought I'd be walking down these stairs forever!"

He raced forward the rest of the way, excited for a change in scenery. Unfortunately for him, when Bacca arrived at the stone archway and looked through it, he saw that the room beyond was even scarier than the stairway.

It was an enormous place, and if there was indeed a ceiling above him it was so high he couldn't see it. The walls were black obsidian, but terrifying bony constructions were everywhere. There were tables and chairs made out of bones, wall decorations made out of bones, and the chandeliers that hung in midair to illuminate the place were entirely made from skulls. Fire burned in their bony eye sockets. Even the giant pillars that seemed to support the room had been crafted in the shape of enormous leg bones. Instead of a traditional base, the sculptor had added bony feet and toes.

"Wow," Bacca said. "This is really something . . ."

Bacca crept deeper into the mysterious room of bones and began to search for Gargantua—still unclear on exactly who or what it might be. The space was so enormous that it would be easy to get lost. The bony decorations also all seemed to look the same. As he made his way, Bacca was careful to keep an eye out for any *movement* in the bones around him. Skeletons were not—all things considered—the most challenging foes to face. But Bacca knew that facing a horde of skeletons out in an open field in the Overworld could be very different than trying to deal with them in confined spaces. On top of this, the creepers had already sent a giant horde of zombies at him as part of their second riddle. Maybe, Bacca thought, this one would involve a horde of skeletons. If even just ten percent of the bones around him suddenly came to life and began acting aggressively, Bacca knew that he would be in big, *big* trouble.

"Maybe there will be very tiny skeletons here," Bacca thought to himself. "And to them, I'm so big that *I'll* be Gargantua. Then the riddle is just asking what I want. Which is of course the Dragon Orb."

Then Bacca said, out loud: "Why is it never that easy?"

"*WHAT?*" boomed an enormous voice in response. The voice was deep and powerful, and the sheer volume of it was enough to hurt Bacca's ears. It shook the smaller bones in the fixtures all around him. The earth seemed to tremble very slightly underneath Bacca's feet.

"Ow," Bacca said, holding his ears. "Could you speak a little more quietly, please?"

There was a silence—probably an annoyed silence—and then the voice came again.

"What Is Never That Easy?" the voice said slowly and deliberately. It was still quite loud, but Bacca had been to louder concerts. He could manage.

"I'm looking for somebody called Gargantua," Bacca said. "I'm solving a riddle. I have to find out what it wants. I was hoping it would be a trick, and Gargantua would turn out to be me. That way, it would be easy."

"I Have Gone By Many Names," the loud voice said. "But Most Now Call Me That One."

"You're Gargantua?" Bacca asked. "Where are you? Are you invisible? All I see in this room is bones."

In response, one of the enormous pillars slowly took a thunderous step in Bacca's direction. Bacca was dumbfounded. He realized that those were its legs. But what exactly was "it"?

"May I Pick You Up?" the thundering voice asked. "The Light Up Here Is Dim. I Cannot See You."

"All right," Bacca said. "Just be gentle."

The loud voice sounded friendly to Bacca . . . but he kept Betty at the ready just in case.

From out of the gloom above came a creaking noise. A giant, skeletal hand extended down from the darkness. The first two fingers curled, making the universal sign for "Come here." Bacca strutted over to the giant hand and climbed aboard. He lit a torch and held it aloft as the hand began to carry him up into the darkness.

By the light of the torch, he spied enormous leg bones, then enormous hips, then an empty rib cage that was larger than most houses. Finally, the huge skeletal arm stopped its ascent when Bacca was in front of the biggest skull he had ever seen.

"Ah," Gargantua said. "You Brought Your Own Light. How Thoughtful."

"You're a skeleton!" Bacca said, stating the obvious. "And—wow!—you're the biggest one I've ever seen! Are all skeletons on this server plane your size?"

The giant skull shook back and forth to indicate no. The sheer wind current generated by this was enough to ruffle Bacca's fur.

"The Others Are Smaller," it said. Bacca thought he detected a note of sadness in the bony giant's voice.

It continued: "Always, They Are Smaller. Like You."

"Are you the skeleton of a giant?" Bacca asked. "I mean, you must be, right?"

The behemoth paused and thought before answering.

"Skeletons Do Not Remember Who We Were Before," it said. "We Only Know Who We Are Now. But I Suppose It Is Likely I Was A Giant."

"Were you—are you—a boy or a girl?" Bacca asked.

"I Have No Recollection," said Gargantua. "I Am Usually Addressed As 'He' . . . But This May Be Done In Error."

"Do you have a bow?" Bacca asked. "Most skeletons have bows."

At this, the giant raised its other hand—the one not holding Bacca—to reveal that indeed it did have a bow. It was the size of a clipper ship, maybe larger. The wood creaked and groaned under its own weight as the huge skeleton held it up.

"Thanks for not shooting me with that," Bacca said. "Most skeletons shoot you on sight."

"I Am Not Like Other Skeletons," Gargantua said.

Then something remarkable happened. Just as Bacca was trying to think of how to bring up the subject of what a giant skeleton might want, Gargantua said:

"I Wish That I Was."

"Excuse me?" Bacca said, cupping his hand to his ear. "What was that? You said that last part very quietly. You know, relatively speaking."

"I Have Become Aware That My Existence Is Not Like What Others Have," it said. "For Other Skeletons, There Are Crafters and Villagers To Hunt. I Have Only The Darkness. Other Skeletons Can Rest During The Day And Come Out At Night. I Have Only The Darkness Of This Place."

"Hmm," Bacca said. "So what you want . . . is to be like other skeletons? To do what they do?"

"If I Could Only Experience It Once," the giant said, "Then I Would Be So Happy."

Bacca had a sinking feeling—unrelated to Gargantua's lowering him back to the floor—that this was going to be how he had to solve the riddle.

Bacca began to puzzle it out. How could such a thing be done?

Bacca's first inclination was to think he should find a way to take the giant skeleton to a place where there were giant humans. Then he would be able to hunt them just like any other skeleton. There were, however, several problems with this. For one, Bacca didn't know where to find giants. True, on this strange server plane, anything was possible. There might be some giants around somewhere, but there also might not. What if Gargantua was a skeleton left over from a society of giants that had gone extinct a thousand years ago? A sad thought, but it was possible.

On top of that, Bacca had no idea how he would go about getting Gargantua out of the giant vault where he lived now. Bacca thought about how exhausting it had been just walking all the steps leading down to this room. Then he imagined crafting all of those steps, and not for somebody his own size, but for a giant! It made Bacca tired just thinking about it. It would also take a very long time. There had to be a quicker way!

Bacca wondered if it would be possible to somehow shrink Gargantua down to the size of a regular skeleton. If he could do that, then the rest would be a snap. Take him out to the surface world and let him do some regular skeleton stuff for a change. That would be easy. But how to shrink something like Gargantua? Bacca did not have any magic of his own. Now that he came to think of it, he had never heard of a witch or wizard that had this power either. And going off and asking around for somebody with magical shrinking skills might be a wild goose chase.

Bacca looked hard for anything he might not have considered yet. There had to be a way to give Gargantua the experience of a normal skeleton. If he couldn't shrink Gargantua down, then maybe . . . just maybe . . .

A possible solution had occurred to Bacca. It would require a whole lot of effort—and he was in no way sure that it would work—but if it did, then the riddle would be solved without needing to shrink Gargantua or find other living giants.

"Hey," Bacca shouted up into the darkness, in the general direction of the giant's skull. "I think I have a way to help you out. But for it to work right, I'm going to need you to close your eyes for a while."

"But I Don't Have Eyes," Gargantua answered.

"In that case, can you turn around and face the wall?" Bacca asked.

"I Can," the giant voice said.

"Thanks," Bacca said. "This might take a while, but I'll work as quickly as I can."

"Don't Worry About That," Gargantua boomed. "I Have Waited Here In This Place For Hundreds Of Years. I Can Wait A Bit More."

Bacca sprang to work. His plan was going to necessitate a good deal of crafting. Not all of the elements were going to be present in a scary place full of obsidian and skeleton bones. He realized that he would need to make a trip back up the long staircase again.

"I'm just going to step out," Bacca told the giant. "But don't worry. I'll be back before you know it. Relatively speaking."

Before Gargantua could answer, Bacca was bounding out of the room and headed back up the long scary staircase.

He didn't want to climb this thing more than once, so as he climbed, Bacca tried to make a mental inventory of all the stuff he would need. Most of the blocks would be shades of black and grey, which were in plentiful abundance down below. But he would also need red sandstone, and lots of it. Luckily for Bacca, he had noticed more than a little of it back at the entrance to the cave where the long stairway had started. The other elements he needed were things he could probably buy or trade for in the village at the center of the rabbit maze.

As Bacca thought more about his plan, the more he became convinced that it might just work. Filled with excitement, Bacca raced faster and faster back up the bony staircase.

There was disagreement among the creepers as to what this development might signify.

"He's not running away, is he?" said one creeper, voicing a concern many of them held. "Giving up and heading home?"

"I don't think so," said another. "That wouldn't make sense. He didn't try to run when Gargantua picked him up. Why would he be scared now?"

"But he's literally running up the staircase," another pointed out.

The creepers looked on and nodded. This fact was clearly true.

"Maybe he's running to something, and not from Gargantua," offered another creeper.

There was a general agreement that either of these could be the case.

"I thought Gargantua was going to step on him," one of the creepers said. "He's so big. Nobody could survive that. One wrong move and squish! That's the end of you."

"Gargantua's not a mean guy, though," one creeper said.

"Yes," agreed another. "In fact he seems quite lonely."

"But he's still a skeleton," another pointed out. "Skeletons like to shoot people with arrows and sometimes smack them with other weapons. There's no getting around that fact."

"I think skeletons go for things their own size," one of the creepers said. "I mean, normal-size skeletons don't spend their time swatting flies or stepping on beetles. So I'm not surprised that Gargantua doesn't want to squish Bacca like a bug."

"I see your point," said another creeper. "Not very sporting, if you did it that way."

"Skeletons have a strong sense of fair play," said another. "Quite admirable, if you ask me."

(Generally, members of hordes were complimentary to other hordes as a matter of professional courtesy. The creepers all believed they were far superior to skeletons—and zombies and witches—but there was a general sense that they were all playing for the same team.)

"Nobody's ever been able to figure out how to help poor Gargantua," one of the creepers said.

"If anybody can figure it out, it will be Bacca," ventured another creeper. "He's done very well so far. Better than most of us expected."

"I hope he figures it out," said another creeper, "for his sake."

"What do you mean by that?" asked another creeper.

"Well, skeletons don't normally step on bugs," said the previous creeper. "But what if a bug really got your hopes up about something . . . and then its plan didn't work?"

"Ah," agreed another creeper. "I certainly might step on *that* bug."

There was a moment of quiet reflection as the creepers collectively imagined this scenario playing out between Bacca and Gargantua.

"But there's no reason to believe that's how it will turn out," one of the creepers finally said. "Bacca hasn't let us down yet. Maybe he's going to do something that will completely surprise us. And Gargantua."

The rest of the creepers hoped that he was right.

Chapter Ten

After a considerable amount of cardio, Bacca finally arrived back at the top of the long, bony staircase. The run should have been exhausting, but he was far too excited to be tired. His plan for Gargantua filled him with new reserves of energy and excitement.

Bacca left the staircase behind and exited through the mouth of the cave. Then he stopped. Falling to one knee, Bacca reached down and ran his fingers through the red sand in front of him. It must have been the leavings of some long-lost mesa biome that had once existed here.

"Perfect," Bacca said to himself, examining the grains of sand. "This will do nicely."

Bacca began gathering all of the red sand and crafting it. For every four blocks of red sand he gathered, he was able to make one block of red sandstone. Then, when he had four blocks of red sandstone, he could craft those into one block of smooth red sandstone.

There was lots and lots of sand at the mouth of the cave. Which was good, Bacca realized. He was going to need all of it.

While Bacca crafted, a small group of curious villagers approached from out of the maze.

"Hello," one of them said.

"Hi there," Bacca said back, continuing to work away.

"We heard that somebody had opened up a new part of the maze," the villager said. "It looks like we heard right!"

"You gotta do what you gotta do," Bacca said, trying to ignore them and focus on his work.

Then a familiar voice asked: "What are you crafting?"

It was the yellow haired boy.

"Something important," Bacca said. "And big. Very big."

"Neat," the boy said. "Can we do anything to help?"

"No," Bacca said, crafting away. "I don't need any—"

Then an idea occurred to him.

"Wait," Bacca said. "You can help, actually."

"Oh good," the yellow haired boy said. "How?"

"I'll need you and a couple of your friends to come with me," Bacca said. "We're going to go down the longest staircase you've ever seen, to a dark place fully of scary bones. And there, we're going to see a skeleton that's as tall as a castle."

The yellow haired boy's eyebrows arched in fear, and he began to open his mouth to object.

"But it'll be a lot of fun!" Bacca quickly added. "I promise."

"Oh," the boy said. "Okay. As long as it's fun."

"I almost have enough smooth red sandstone," Bacca said. "But there are two other things I'm going to need for this plan to work. Two other things I'm going to need *a lot* of. Maybe you can help me find them."

"Sure," said the yellow haired boy. "What are they?"

"The first is torches," Bacca said.

"That's no problem," the boy replied. "We've got plenty of those in our village. If there's one thing you need to have plenty of lying around in a subterranean village, it's torches!"

"Good," Bacca said. "The other thing is gold. I will need quite a bit of it."

When Bacca said this, the faces of some of the villagers turned to frowns.

"What?" Bacca asked, feeling confused. "Do you have something against gold?"

They shook their heads no.

"We know where to get lots of gold," the boy said brightly.

The other villagers continued to frown. One of them put a hand on the boy's shoulder to quiet him down. It was clear they didn't like this topic.

"What?" Bacca said again, still not understanding the concern.

"There *is* a gold mine hidden in the maze," said one of the villagers. "But it is not a place you would want to go. We stay away from it."

Bacca said: "Wait . . . I feel like I walked through your entire maze when I was making my map, and I never saw a gold mine."

"All the same, it's there," a villager said.

"I can show you!" the yellow haired boy added brightly.

Several of the villagers shushed him.

"What?" the boy said. "It's true. I can!"

"Why don't you want me to see your gold mine?" Bacca asked. "I promise not to take more gold than I need for my riddle. And trust me, it's *very* important that I solve this riddle."

"You misunderstand," the villager said. "We're not worried about you stealing our gold. We're concerned for you—for your safety—just as we would be concerned for the safety of *anyone* who went inside the mine."

"Oh yeah?" Bacca said. "This may surprise you, but I've faced all kinds of monsters before, in all kinds of mines."

"I'm sure you have," said the villager nervously. "But this cave is different. Its . . . *haunted.*"

The rest of the villagers nodded in grim agreement.

"What?" Bacca said. "Haunted? Really?"

"*I'm* not afraid of the ghost," the yellow haired boy asserted loudly. "Other people are, but I'm not."

Bacca smiled.

"Well, maybe you can show me where the mine is . . . if your friends here are too scared," Bacca said. "Though I can't believe that out of all these people, the only brave one would be a little boy."

"That's easy for you to say," a villager replied.

"You'll be scared too," another villager said. "You'll be scared once you see it!"

"Somehow, I seriously doubt that," said Bacca, recalling some of his hairiest adventures and thinking that the likelihood that whoever or whatever guarded this mine might top them was infinitesimally small.

When Bacca had finished constructing his blocks of smooth red sandstone, he followed the villagers back to their village in the center of the maze. Here, he was given all the torches that he could carry.

"Thank you," Bacca said. "These will work perfectly."

"We've discussed it, and we agree to take you to the gold mine," one of the villagers said. "But don't say we didn't warn you."

"Okay," Bacca said with a grin. "I won't."

The villagers took Bacca on a winding course through the maze, with the yellow haired boy leading the way.

"Gee," Bacca observed, "maybe I *didn't* come this way when I was making my map. It certainly looks different than anything I remember."

The villagers stopped in front of a small opening to the side of the passage. It wasn't very large. Bacca reckoned that if you were going quickly— and, say, only interested in finding a witch or a green rabbit—you might not even notice it at all.

"This is the gold mine," one of the villagers told him. "But please, be careful. The ghost inside is definitely scary."

"Thanks for the warning," Bacca said, and crawled through the opening.

By the light of his torch, he saw that he was in a large, long room. The ground was rough and uneven. There were long veins of gold ore running everywhere, but no ghost that he could see.

So Bacca took out his iron pickaxe and got to work.

He would need a lot of gold to solve the riddle of Gargantua, but this place looked like it had hardly been mined at all. The ore was just there waiting to be taken. It was almost too good to be true.

Bacca mined one vein until it was entirely dry, then started in on another, and then another after that. He got into a rhythm and actually started enjoying the hard work. He certainly didn't see what all the fuss was about. There didn't seem to be any ghosts. There weren't even spiders or bats. As subterranean mines went, it was downright friendly.

Then, suddenly, he heard it.

"Boooooo."

One long, ghostly note echoed across the mine.

Bacca thought it was the villagers playing a joke on him.

"Real funny guys," he called back, not *that* easily rattled. "But seriously, this is a great mine. Thank you for taking me here. I'm going to have more than enough gold to—"

Bacca stopped mid-sentence.

A glowing blue-white shape was drifting toward him from out of the deepest reaches of the mine. It slowly drew closer with every second that passed. It gradually took the shape of a villager with a skeletal face.

"Boooo!" it cried, loudly and insistently.

Bacca had faced almost every manner of monster, but never a ghost. Would it be friendly? Would it be angry? Would he take damage if it touched him? As the incandescent spirit floated nearer, Bacca was too curious to think of preparing for battle, or to even be scared. He did not even set down his pickaxe. As he watched in amazement, the ghost drifted up until it stood toe-to-toe with him.

"Boooo!" it said again.

"Hello," Bacca said, hoping that a cheerful demeanor might set the two of them off on the right foot. "Lovely mine you have here. Hope you don't mind me taking just a little gold from it. Or a lot, I guess. Because, um, actually I'm taking a lot."

The ghost looked at Bacca. An expression of puzzlement crossed its translucent face. Then it moaned again.

"Boooo."

"Yes," Bacca said. "I heard you the first time."

The ghost waved its hand at Bacca, almost as though it was casting a spell. Bacca was at first unsure what was happening, but suddenly noticed himself feeling a whole lot lighter. He opened his inventory and realized that all of his newly-mined gold ore was gone. He looked down at the floor of the mine, and saw that the ore had been magically returned to the earth.

"My gold!" Bacca cried. "What's the big idea?"

"Boooo," said the ghost in a self-satisfied tone.

"Dang it," Bacca said. "It's never easy, is it? Do you say anything other than 'boo'? That would be helpful."

The ghost shook its head and smiled from cheekbone to cheekbone.

"Of course not. Hmm . . . well look, I need this gold," Bacca said. "I've got to solve a riddle to help the dragons recover their orb. And I need this gold to do that."

"Boooo?" said the ghost, in a tone that managed to get across the attitude of 'So what's that got to do with me?'

"Look, it's not like you *need* this gold, right?" Bacca said. "You're not *using* it for anything at the moment."

The ghost bobbed up and down silently for a moment.

"So what if . . ." Bacca said, trying to think of a solution.

Then an idea struck him.

"What if I bring it back when I'm done?" Bacca asked.

The ghost said, "Booo?" It had clearly never heard such an absurd proposition.

"Hear me out," Bacca said. "I only need this gold ore for a little while. I have to craft it into something. Then I have to take it down to the skeletal place where Gargantua lives and kind of . . . use it as a prop."

"Booo?"

"The details aren't important," Bacca continued. "The important thing is that once I'm done, I'm done. I won't need the gold anymore. Gargantua won't need it either. I could just bring it all back to you. Or the villagers could. How does that sound?"

"Booo . . ." said the ghost carefully, thinking it over.

Eventually, it nodded at Bacca. Maybe it liked the idea after all.

But then the ghost pointed to the entrance to the mine where the yellow haired boy and the other villagers were still waiting, just out of sight. The ghost raised both its arms aggressively and make a scary face.

"*BOOOOOO!!!*"

"Ahh, I think I understand," Bacca said. "You're a scary ghost. You've got a reputation to keep. I get it. Don't worry—I'll be sure to tell the villagers you were absolutely terrifying."

Bacca did an impression of a person who was very scared, knocking at the knees and chattering his teeth.

"Booo!" roared the ghost in glee, slapping its thigh. It liked that a lot.

The ghost stuck one bluish, slightly-transparent hand forward. Bacca reached out to shake on their agreement. There was a moment of awkwardness as Bacca's hand passed right through it, so he simply moved his hand up and down over the ghost's hand, in the closest approximation he could think of to a proper business handshake. The ghost smiled in appreciation. A moment later, Bacca felt his inventory filling back up with all the gold he had mined.

"Thank you," Bacca said. "And don't worry, a deal's a deal. I won't let you down."

Bacca closed his eyes and took a deep breath, readying himself like an actor at an audition.

Then he screamed: "Aaaaaaaah!"

Bacca winked at the ghost. The ghost nodded and clapped its hands, appearing to enjoy this very much.

"Aaaaah!" Bacca screamed again. "There's totally a big scary ghost in here!"

The ghost jumped up and down with pleasure. Or maybe floated. It was hard for Bacca to know for sure, but he waved goodbye to the ghost and hurried out of the mine.

The villagers looked on anxiously as Bacca emerged, doing his best to appear terrified and white as a sheet . . . inasmuch as that was possible for someone entirely covered in brown fur.

"That's a real ghost in there!" Bacca cried in alarm. He allowed this half-truth to sit, and did not include the fact that he and the specter had actually got along rather well.

"We told you so," said one of the villagers.

"Do you believe us *now*?!" said another.

"I certainly do," said Bacca. "But don't worry. I barely escaped, but I was able to mine all the gold I needed before it appeared. We just have to, er, bring it back after."

"Bring it back?" asked one of the villagers. "What?"

"Yeah," said Bacca, thinking quickly on its feet. "If we don't, what if the ghost is so mad that it decides to come out from the cave and haunt the entire village? I don't think we want to risk that . . ." The villagers quickly shook their heads in agreement. "But don't worry about it right now. We're all good for the moment. Now I just need a few volunteers. I think three people would be enough."

"Ooh, me, me!" cried the yellow haired boy.

"That's one," said Bacca. "Anybody else? Say, you two look about right."

He had pointed out a blacksmith and a farmer from among the group of villagers, and after just a little cajoling (it didn't hurt to remind them that the gold had already been taken, so it was in the village's best interest to return it as quickly as possible), he convinced them to join his group.

Bacca and the three villagers walked back through the maze until they once again stood at the sandy cave entrance (not so sandy anymore, thanks to Bacca's harvesting). They passed through it and headed down the dark staircase that lay beyond. As the blocks around them began to grow increasingly bony and morbid, the yellow haired boy began to shake with fear.

"Are you sure we're going to be safe down here?" he asked Bacca.

"Yes," Bacca said. "I'll give you a few reasons why. One, I've been down here before and there's nothing much to be frightened of. There are all these bones but there aren't any skeletons . . . at least not any that are going to attack you. Two . . ."

Here, Bacca took Betty out of his inventory and let it glisten in the torchlight.

"If anything *did* show up," Bacca continued, "it wouldn't live very long. Three . . . and maybe most importantly . . . *I'm Bacca.* I always find a way to win."

"Okay," the boy said, and he stopped shaking quite so much. "That *does* make me feel better."

They continued down, down, down the seemingly endless staircase. The oppressive décor of obsidian and bone never relented.

"This is a very strange place," noted the blacksmith.

"It's about to get even stranger," Bacca said.

Moments later, they reached the bony room at the bottom of the staircase. The yellow haired boy and the other villagers crept inside warily, examining the bone amenities with great caution. Bacca saw that Gargantua had not moved. His giant feet still faced the wall. (As, presumably, did the rest of him—unseen in the darkness above.)

"Hello, Gargantua," Bacca called. "I'm back and I brought some friends. We're going to get started on this project. But still no peeking, right?"

A thunderous voice shook the room.

"I Remember," it said. "No Peeking."

"Good," pronounced Bacca, and he set to work organizing the villagers.

"What on earth was that voice?" the farmer asked.

"Oh, sorry," said Bacca. "That was Gargantua. He's . . ."

Bacca decided it might be too frightening for the villagers to learn that he was addressing a skeleton as large as a castle (they seemed like they would take the news much worse than the boy had), and that the pillars appearing to hold up an unseen ceiling were actually its legs.

Instead, Bacca said: "He's . . . got his head in the clouds right now. Don't worry, you'll probably get to see more of him later."

"Okay," said the yellow haired boy, though it was clear he knew just what was going on. Then he shouted: "*Hi, Gargantua!*"

"Hello," came the great voice thundering back. "Pleased To Meet You, Stranger."

Bacca ushered the villagers to the side of the room and began to position them.

"Okay . . ." Bacca began. "Blacksmith, I want you to stand here. Pretend that you're just now leaving your shop. You've worked a little too late, and nightfall has caught you unaware. It's a situation that makes you nervous. Good. Exactly right. Farmer? Stand here. Can you make an expression like you've just seen something scary? That's good, but even scarier. Even scarier! Perfect!"

Finally, Bacca turned to the yellow haired boy.

"Can you turn to the side and point, like you're trying to warn people about something dangerous?" Bacca asked.

"Sure!" the boy said enthusiastically. "But wait . . . Why are we doing this again?"

"You're going to be my artist models," said Bacca. "I'm going to build versions of you out of blocks. But you're going to be big. Really, really big."

"What?" said the farmer.

"Why would you do that?" said the blacksmith.

"Awesome!" said the yellow haired boy.

Bacca told the group that they would just have to trust him. Then he started to craft.

For Bacca's plan to work, he was going to have to create versions of these villagers that were in proportion to Gargantua. He had intentionally selected villagers with darker clothing that would be easy to duplicate on a larger scale out of the blocks available in the room. Villager skin was a strange, indeterminate color, but Bacca had realized that in the shadows cast in this room, smooth red sandstone would look about right. Bacca used obsidian and stone for most of the clothing, and improvised for the rest.

"That doesn't look anything like me," the farmer protested as Bacca worked away.

"I've only done your feet so far," Bacca barked back. "And it looks *exactly* like your feet."

"I'd have to agree," the blacksmith said, peering at the farmer's feet.

"That's . . ." the farmer stammered, looking at the giant pile of obsidian that Bacca had amassed across the room. "That's *only* my feet!? Most *houses* are smaller than that! How big do you plan on making me?"

"Right," said Bacca. "So now maybe you understand why I needed so much crafting material. Now, please be perfectly still. As you can see, I'm not even close to done."

Bacca worked and worked and worked. If anyone anywhere had ever created a larger statue of three villagers, Bacca didn't know about it. Now and then his energy flagged and he started to think about resting, but then his thoughts turned back to the dragon orb—and how important it was to the dragons—and rediscovered the motivation to keep on working.

"Hey!" said the yellow haired boy. "That's starting to look like me. My statue will be done first!"

"That's because you're shortest," Bacca replied. "There's less of you to craft."

"Oh," the boy said. "I guess that makes sense."

Soon, Bacca was entirely finished with the boy's statue. It loomed above them, its head nearly lost in the darkness above. As a finishing touch, Bacca smelted some gold from the gold ore he'd taken, and used it to recreate the color of the boy's hair.

"So *that's* why you needed the gold," the yellow haired boy said.

"That's why I needed *some* of the gold," Bacca corrected him.

The hours flew by, and soon Bacca had finished his three massive sculptures. They looked exactly like the farmer, the blacksmith, and the yellow haired boy—with the sole exception of being about a hundred times larger in every way. For a moment, Bacca thought it would be a pity that so few people would get to see these creations. Usually, when he worked this hard on something, an audience of thousands would come and view it. Then he remembered the riddle again, and decided it was okay if these objects had a very small audience . . . as long as they served an important purpose.

"Whew," said the farmer. "Glad you're done. I was getting positively exhausted holding that pose."

"*You're* exhausted?" said the boy. "Think about how Bacca must feel. He had to build three big statues!"

"I suppose you have a point," said the farmer.

Bacca couldn't stop to reflect on his work, because he was still not finished with everything. There was more to do.

He smelted the rest of the gold ore from his inventory into gold ingots. Then he crafted these into enormous blocks of gold. When he had several hundred gold blocks, he built a temporary stone staircase that took him up the side of the wall until he was even higher than the statues of the villagers.

"Hello!" called the yellow haired boy. "What are you doing up there? You're so high, we can't even see you!"

"Just wait," came the reply from way up high. "You'll find out in a minute."

From his perch, Bacca began to position the gold blocks into the wall until they formed a giant circular disc.

"Now I can see something!" the boy observed from below. "It's huge! It looks like the sun!"

"Good," Bacca said. "It's supposed to."

"When have *you* ever seen the sun?" the blacksmith asked the boy accusingly. "We live in a village in a subterranean dungeon maze."

"My family sells rabbit stew topside on the weekends," the boy answered. "There's a farmers market. It's very nice."

The blacksmith grumbled. He had probably never seen the actual sun himself, and was jealous.

Beneath his literally golden sun, Bacca built a long ledge of stone. Onto this ledge, he began to place the torches he had obtained in the village. Soon there were two piles of them, each ready to burst into flame at the smallest urging.

"Okay," Bacca said, returning to ground level. "I think we're finally set. Villagers? I've really appreciated your help, but for your own safety it's probably best if you leave now. If you want to watch what happens, maybe just go over through the doorway by the staircase, out of harm's way."

The villagers were obviously curious—especially the yellow haired boy—but they did not need to be told twice to relocate for their own safety. Soon, they stood back at the entrance to the room, peering inside at Bacca.

"Now," Bacca said, "can you hear me, Gargantua?"
An enormous "Yes" ricocheted back.

"Good," said Bacca. "We're about to begin. What I've done is create a kind of 'skeleton simulator.' It will allow a skeleton of your proportions to experience—just for a few moments—what it's like to be a regular-sized skeleton up on the surface of the Overworld."

"I Am Excited To Begin," Gargantua said. Small tremors shook the floor as the behemoth shifted its weight back and forth on its heels in anticipation.

"I'm going to give you a series of instructions," said Bacca. "I need you to follow them exactly."

"Yes," said Gargantua. "I Will Do So. Let Us Begin."

There was more excited trembling. Bits of dust fell from the ceiling of the room.

"I know you're anxious to start, but wait just a second," Bacca said, racing back up the staircase to the ledge that held the torches.

Bacca struck a flint to one of the piles, and it caught easily. In mere instants, all the torches in the pile burned brightly. Their flames were reflected in the giant gold disc on the wall. Because of that reflection, for the first time ever, the entirety of the enormous bony chamber was illuminated. Bacca looked out and saw the full body of Gargantua—who had to be the largest skeleton in existence—still dutifully facing the wall.

"Ack!" the giant cried. "What's Happening To My Eyes? The Light! I've Never Seen So Much Light! It Burns."

Bacca smiled. Gargantua wasn't even looking directly at the flames.

"This is daytime," Bacca narrated. "The time that all good skeletons fear. A big, hot ball is floating in the sky creating this awful stuff called sunlight, which burns skeletons to a crisp. Can you feel the heat?"

"Ahh," said Gargantua. "I Can. It Is Horrible! Horrible!"

"Yes," said Bacca. "But you are safe. Like any smart skeleton, you are hiding under the earth. You spend half your time here. But you're not sleeping. No way! You're waiting. You're carefully planning your next attack. You're thinking about all those crafters and villagers and other people who you're going to be shooting with arrows once the moon is out. It's all you think about. It's your all-consuming obsession."

"Yes! Yes!" cried the towering skeleton. "I Want To Shoot Them With My Arrows. I Want To Hear Them Screaming And Running Away. I Want That So Bad!"

Gargantua's giant bony fingers gripped his bow tightly. There was a sound like the hull of a wooden ship straining under the force of a typhoon. Bacca wondered how many trees—a small forest of them!—had been sacrificed to craft a bow of that size.

"Now the sun is beginning to set," Bacca said. "The day is ending. Soon it will be time to pop out of the ground and go on the attack!"

"Yes!" said Gargantua, growing excited. "It's Going To Be Great. I'm Going To Shoot So Many People With My Bow!"

From his spot on the platform, Bacca gradually began to extinguish the torches that burned underneath the great golden sun. He went slowly and methodically, snuffing them out one by one. Sunsets in the Overworld passed quickly, so Bacca did not draw the process out any longer than he had to. Soon only a few smoldering torches remained, and he planned to keep them going to simulate the faint light cast by the moon.

"Now the sun is down!" Bacca cried. "It's night! It's the time when all skeletons should rise from the earth and shoot their bows."

"Yes!" Gargantua boomed. "This Is Awesome! Yes! Yes!"

There was an awkward silence, broken only by the crackling of the torches.

"So . . . now you should rise from the grave," Bacca said. Gargantua didn't move though, and Bacca realized that never having done this before, he probably didn't even know how. "And of course the way you would do that is by turning around!"

"Oh," the enormous skeleton said. "Right. Sorry."

Ka-*Chung*. Ka-*Chung*. Ka-*Chung*.

Gargantua took several slow, deliberate steps as it turned around to face Bacca. The cavernous room shook under its weight. The enormous skeleton's bony eye sockets scanned the area for a suitable target.

"There, look to your left!" cried Bacca. "A villager! A farmer, by the looks of it. He would make an excellent target for your bow."

The skeleton slowly swiveled its skull toward the towering statue that Bacca had built of the farmer. It was roughly the same size as Gargantua.

"Yes!" Gargantua cried. "A Target!"

While the huge skeleton did not have lips to speak of, Bacca had the distinct impression that Gargantua was now smiling.

The skeleton reached over its shoulder to a quiver. From it, the creature pulled an arrow that was longer than the tallest of trees. It notched the arrow with a loud *thud*! It pulled back on the bowstring. There was a sudden tension in the air, as if the whole world was holding its breath. Gargantua took careful aim at the lifelike sculpture, and let the arrow fly.

There was a whooshing sound as the arrow launched across the room. Bacca had the sensation of someone standing closer than recommended to the incoming path of an airplane. The arrow struck the statue on the nose. The enormous construction wobbled back and forth.

"A direct hit!" said Bacca. "A few more like that, and he'll be done for."

"Yes!" Gargantua returned. "Done For!"

The skeleton pulled another arrow from its quiver and fired. Then another. The statue of the farmer tumbled over. There was a deafening sound like a small building collapsing as it fell to the floor.

"Hooray!" Gargantua said. "I Feel So Alive!" Then after a moment, added: "Relatively Speaking."

"Now look over there!" Bacca called out. "That looks like a blacksmith. He must have seen what you did to the farmer, because he looks really nervous. And you're going to give him a reason to be nervous, right?"

"Yes!" said Gargantua, swiveling its skull to locate the blacksmith. "Yes, I Am."

The skeleton methodically drew arrow after arrow and sent them flying across the room. There was a great clamoring as the statue went tumbling to the floor. The impact sent blocks flying. A cloud of dust began to rise from the floor.

"But wait," Bacca cried. "You're not done yet. There's a little boy from the village. Look at him!

He's pointing at you. Are you going to let him get away with that?"

"NO!" Gargantua cried, in a voice so loud it caused the ceiling to shake. "No I'm Not!"

The skeleton swiveled around to face the statue of the boy. Being smaller, it took Gargantua only two arrows to knock it over. It hit the ground and broke apart with a loud, blocky *Ker-Splat!*

"Nice work," Bacca called from his perch. "You really showed those villagers. They're going to think twice before they mess with skeletons again."

"They Will Think Twice," agreed the giant.

"But . . . uh-oh, what's happening?" Bacca asked rhetorically as he began to light the second pile of torches. "It looks like night is over. The sun is starting to come back out. The awful, nasty, mean sun that likes to burn skeletons into little blackened crisps!"

"Ack!" Gargantua said. "Oh No!"

"Quick," Bacca said. "Now is the time to go back under the ground. To rest and meditate on all the good shooting you just did. To anticipate all the exciting hunts that are yet to come."

"Good, Yes," the giant agreed. "I Will Do That."

Remembering himself, Gargantua took several thunderous steps, rotating until he was once again facing the wall. The torches burned brightly, reflected in the enormous golden sun. Bacca turned and saw the *real* villagers watching from the doorway. The yellow haired boy smiled and gave Bacca a thumbs-up. Bacca gave him a thumbs-up back.

Then he held his breath.

Now was the moment of truth.

In the dark ledges hidden in the shadowy corners of the ceiling, there was suddenly a great murmuration. ("Great" in this case meant it was heard by a few nearby sleeping bats who had really excellent, radar-like hearing.)

"This is quite remarkable," one of the creepers was saying. "There were several ways to approach this problem, granted, but I never would have expected him to do *this*."

"That looked like fun," another creeper idly mused. "Sometimes I wish *I* was a skeleton. Shooting bows has to be very exciting!"

"Perhaps, but it is certainly *not* better than sneaking up on people and exploding!" warned a senior creeper.

The creepers nodded in unison, then turned their attention back to the scene unfolding below them.

"Those statues Bacca built were the biggest I've ever seen," a creeper said. "And they really and truly looked like villagers. That is, before Gargantua destroyed them."

"Do you think he's going to buy it?" a different creeper asked. "I mean, all Bacca did was just sort of *simulate* what a skeleton could do."

"Maybe so," said another creeper, "but it sure was a *good* simulation. When Gargantua was shooting arrows at those statues, I felt for a second like he *was* a regular-sized skeleton. Then I thought, if he's regular-sized, then maybe I'm just a very small creeper. It really messed with my head!"

"Probably, it's better not to think about stuff like that," an experienced creeper pointed out. "You could make yourself crazy."

There was much head shaking in agreement.

Then a creeper said, "If Bacca passes this test . . . if Gargantua agrees he's solved the riddle . . . then there's only one riddle left. Only one until . . . Until . . ."

The thought was so exciting that the creeper could not complete the sentence. None of the creepers could.

Instead, they sat in rapt silence, watching to see what happened next.

As the last of the torches began to burn out, Bacca descended the stone stairs from his platform. He reached the floor and walked back over to where the bony giant was still facing the wall. Although the skeleton was demonstrably without lungs, Bacca could have sworn he heard the giant breathing hard.

Gargantua noticed Bacca and turned back around to face him.

"That Was Good," the great skeleton said, slowly and ponderously. "Very Good. I Never Thought I Would Be Able To Do What Other Skeletons Can. Thank You."

"You're welcome," said Bacca, hoping that all of this work was going to have a payoff.

"The Creepers Said I Should Help You If You Gave Me What I Truly Desired," said Gargantua. "That Is Exactly What You Have Done. Accordingly, I Will Show You The Way Forward."

"Thank you," said Bacca. "I appreciate that."

"But . . ." the bony giant hesitated. "I Am Concerned. There Is Only One In That Direction. There Is Only . . . *Her.*"

Bacca didn't like the sound of that.

"Her?" Bacca said.

"I Suppose That You Will Meet Her Soon Enough," the Skeleton said. "But People Are Always Upset When They Return From Seeing Her. They Are Often Sad. Sometimes, They Are Even Injured.

I Think Seeing Her Must Be A Bad Idea. But The Creepers Said It Was Where You Would Desire To Go. I Will Not Keep You From Your Heart's Desire, Especially When You Have Just Given Me Mine. Now Then, Are You Ready To Go To Her?"

"Um, just a second," Bacca said.

He rushed over to the doorway where the villagers still lingered expectantly.

"Guys, I have a big favor to ask," Bacca said. "That sun up there made out of blocks of gold . . . it needs to go back to the haunted mine. Do you think you could do that for me? I made a promise to the ghost."

"A promise to the ghost?" said the farmer, as if such an idea was outrageous.

"Why would you do something like *that*?" said the blacksmith.

"It was the only way I could get the ghost to agree to let me leave with the gold," Bacca said. "Otherwise, he would use his magic to take it out of my inventory and put it back in the ground."

But the yellow haired boy, who was clever enough to understand what had happened all along, said: "Sure. We'll help you keep your promise, won't we?"

The other two villagers grudgingly agreed that they would also help.

"And please tell the ghost I'm sorry I couldn't come personally," Bacca said. "Actually, scratch that. I think it would make him happiest if you just screamed when you saw him, dropped the gold, and ran away. He likes it when people are afraid. He won't hurt you. Quite a nice chap, actually. Just don't let on that you know."

Bidding the villagers farewell, Bacca returned to the foot of the giant.

"Okay then," Bacca called. "I'm ready to go."

"Good," Gargantua said. "I Am Ready To Take You."

The giant bent down and held its bony hand flat against the floor. Bacca stepped onto the hand and held onto the gigantic thumb for balance.

Gargantua lifted him up and began to take the first of several enormous steps across the room.

"Where are we going, exactly?" Bacca asked.

"Not Far," the giant replied.

The giant reached the far side of the room and lifted Bacca to a ledge near the ceiling. It was a small ledge, but big enough for Bacca to stand comfortably. The moment his foot touched it, the bricks in the wall beside the ledge magically parted, and a new passageway was revealed.

"She Is Through There," Gargantua said as Bacca peered into the gloom beyond. "I Have Never Met Her, But If I Were You . . . I Would Be Careful."

"Thanks," said Bacca.

"The Thanks Goes To You," Gargantua said. "You Allowed Me To Know The World As Other Skeletons Know It, If Only For A Few Moments. If I Can Ever Repay Your Kindness, You Have Only To Ask."

With this, the behemoth turned its huge bulk around and stalked back across the room. Looking down from his spot on the ledge, Bacca saw the villagers beginning to disassemble the enormous gold sun, block by block. Satisfied that his work was finished here, he walked into the tunnel beside the ledge . . . and toward whatever—or whomever—might lie beyond.

CHAPTER ELEVEN

Bacca headed down the dark corridor. There was an old, musty smell. It was deathly quiet. Nothing stirred.

As Bacca progressed, the pathway before him widened and eventually opened into a small clearing. On the far side of the clearing was a wall made out of quartz. In the center of the wall was a quartz door. And beside the door was a very tiny building, barely big enough for one person to stand inside. And yet that's just what someone was doing!

Bacca now realized it was a guardhouse with a guard. The guard looked like a typical villager, except he wore a fancy red-and-blue uniform with gold buttons and a high circular hat.

As Bacca approached, the guard grew excited— but not in an unfriendly way—smiled, and took out a tray made of chiseled quartz, with a quartz dome covering it. He held this tray out to his new guest.

"You must be Bacca!" the guard said in a friendly tone. "They told me you might get this far. Well, not so much told as whispered it so quietly I could hardly hear. But enough about them right? I'm supposed to give this to you."

And with that, the guard plucked the dome from off the chiseled quartz tray. Underneath was a single mycelium block with writing on it. The guard smiled brightly.

"Thank you," said Bacca. He leaned in to read the inscription.

Through this door is the Tinkerer
You will be pleased to know that she is relatively harmless.
The same cannot be said for her creations.
Some believe her workshop is filled with monstrosities.
The Tinkerer would disagree.
Who is right and who is wrong?

When he finished reading, Bacca motioned to the guard that he could replace the dome.

"It's so exciting to finally have you here!" the guard said, covering the block back up. "There was no guarantee you'd come. But I'm so glad that you did! Makes my job much more interesting!"

"What exactly am I in for?" Bacca asked. "Who is the Tinkerer?"

"Search me," the guard said.

"Wait . . . you mean you don't know?" Bacca asked. "The riddle on the block seems to say she's just through this door."

"Ooh, it's a *she*?" the guard said. "Now we are learning things, aren't we?"

"Huh?" Bacca said.

"Hey, I'm just a guard," said the guard. "I stand here and guard the place. That's what I do. I don't really keep tabs on what's inside."

"Do you mean you don't know anything about what I'm going to find on the other side of this door?" Bacca said, frustrated that a man in his position wasn't more inquisitive about the work he was doing.

Suddenly, the guard's face grew very thoughtful and serious.

"Very few people go through that door," he said. "And they always come out in a bad mood, like they've really been let down. Or worse! Of course, I can't think about that too much! Got to stay positive in a job like this. It's too depressing to think you might be guarding a place that made people sad."

"I see," Bacca said. "Thank you. I think."

"You're welcome," the guard said brightly.

"One more question," Bacca said. "How did you get this job? Why do you stay here guarding this door?"

"I have to," said the guard. "*They* want me to."

"Who is 'they'?" asked Bacca.

"The creepers, obviously," said the guard. "I lost a bet with them. It was a long, long time ago. The moral of my story is: don't make bets with creepers. Anyhow, they gave me two choices. And I chose this one. To be a guard until such time as somebody comes to relieve me. It's no picnic standing here all day, but it certainly beats the alternative."

"Were they going to kill you?" Bacca asked.

"*Kill me!*" the guard said in alarm, putting his hand over his mouth. "What said anything about killing!? No! How dreadful!"

"Sorry," Bacca said. "I just assumed . . ."

"Goodness, no," said the guard. "The other choice was to marry a creeper. Or maybe it was a creeper's daughter. I forget. Anyway, they all look the same to me. All square and purple. Not my type, you know?"

"In my biome, they're green," Bacca said. "But they're still jerks."

"You can say that again," agreed the guard.

Bacca said goodbye to the guard and opened the door in the quartz wall. Beyond it were quartz stairs leading up.

"It's always stairs in this place," Bacca said to himself with a sigh, and started climbing.

As it turned out, he did not have far to go.

After ascending only a few flights, the staircase ended in what was clearly a crafter's workshop. It was filled with items that Bacca knew well. They were all things that he had crafted himself at one time or another. There were clocks and minecarts and rails and pressure plates. There were suits of armor and tools. There were bookshelves and chests and compasses.

But all of them—each one of the objects inside of this room—were profoundly *wrong*. Bacca was sure of it . . . without really knowing how he knew. He just *knew*.

Wrong.

All of the items were somehow deeply incorrect. Bacca had never seen so many wrong things in one place before. It was a strange sensation, and one that he felt more with his gut than with his head.

Bacca crept deeper into the workshop. After being inside so many ridiculously big rooms within the creeper fortress, it was refreshing to be in a place that was at least normally sized. There were torches burning in braziers on the walls, and there was also a skylight in the ceiling where the sun shone through. (Bacca realized he must now be near the very top of the creeper fortress.) In the back of the workshop were several doors, but all of them were closed.

Bacca turned back to the items on the workshop tables, and tried to figure out where this strange feeling of *wrongness* was coming from.

On the nearest table was a regular-looking detector rail. Bacca knew these items well, and had crafted them many times before. A complex but not overly-complex device, you could build them with six iron ingots, a redstone, and a stone pressure plate. And all of those elements seemed to be represented in the finished product on the table in front of him.

And yet . . .

Bacca picked the device up and examined it more closely. Detector rails were supposed to send signals whenever minecarts crossed them. But by examining the wiring, Bacca could tell that this one was going to send signals all the time for no reason. It wouldn't work at all.

Bacca set down the detector rail and picked up the item beside it. It was another rail. More specifically, it was a powered rail crafted from gold ingots, redstone, and a wooden stick. Bacca turned it over in his hands and held it up to the sunlight streaming through the skylight. The red and orange center of the rail shimmered in the light . . . but not *quite* in the normal way. Suddenly, a horrible realization struck Bacca, and he almost dropped the device. This thing in his hand could be deadly!

Most powered rails sped up minecarts in a useful and helpful way. When you were moving around carts full of stuff, a little extra zip was just what you wanted. But *this* powered rail had been *over-*powered. It would send carts careening off at an unsafe speed. Maybe they would fly off the track entirely. And what would happen to the innocent people they crashed into?

Bacca didn't like to imagine it.

Setting down the rail, Bacca moved to a different table of items. Here was a collection of fireworks. At first glance, they all looked to have been crafted in the normal way. But when he looked more closely, something about their construction was definitely off. Bacca picked one of them up and carefully unscrewed the top. Peering inside, he was shocked to see that someone had packed in ten times as much gunpowder as was needed. This was not so much a firework as a missile. A missile that might explode and hurt somebody.

Bacca moved to yet another table. This one was covered with material for making fishing rods— all kinds of sticks and strings—along with several finished rods. As a lifelong enthusiast of raw fish, Bacca knew a thing or two about fishing rods. He could tell right away that anybody who used *these* rods was going to end up with more than just wet pants and no fish. The weight on these rods was off-kilter. This meant if you weren't careful when casting your line, you'd end up falling forward, probably falling into water. But not everybody could swim! (And even if you could swim, lakes and rivers on the Overworld could be filled with nasty, tentacle-y things with beaks and teeth.)

Bacca continued from table to table, moving through the workshop. At every turn, he found another category of items that were bad, wrong, and dangerous.

"Whoever this Tinkerer is, she's got a lot to answer for . . ." Bacca said to himself.

Suddenly, there was a noise at the back of the workshop. One of the doors opened, and through it walked one of the strangest people Bacca had ever seen.

She was not much taller than Bacca, but was almost perfectly round. She wore a large flat hat made out of iron. From the brim of the hat dangled a series of long metal tubes with prisms at the ends. Were they microscopes? Kaleidoscopes? Some . . . other kind of scopes? Bacca had no idea. The strange woman also wore several tool belts, and a large backpack full of crafting materials. Whenever she took a step, she clanked loudly.

"Ha!" she announced. "What do we have here?"

She squinted through her tubes at Bacca—trying one tube after another—but never quite seeming to find the right one.

"Another *supplicant*, I suppose?" she muttered to herself. "A *hairy* supplicant."

"What's a supplicant?" Bacca asked.

"Somebody who wants something from me," the woman said. "They *always* want something. And I give them what they want, but they're never pleased. And still they keep coming! And here you are! Another one!"

"You must be the Tinkerer, right?" Bacca said, trying to size this strange lady up.

"See?" the woman returned. "*Supplicant!* I knew it! Yes, I'm the one you're looking for."

"Pleased to meet you," Bacca said. "I'm Bacca."

"You're name's not important," the Tinkerer said rudely. "Yap yap yap. All you supplicants ever do is yap. Just tell me what you want, and I'll see what I can find."

Bacca considered his next move carefully. He wanted to test the water, so to speak. Who was this odd woman? Why did she have such a bad attitude? And why did she craft all of these horrible things?

"I'm not exactly sure what I want yet," Bacca said deceptively. "I'm still trying to make up my mind."

"Typical," the Tinkerer said. "Supplicants can *never* decide on something quickly."

"Yes," Bacca said. "Anyway, maybe we could look around? That might help me get some ideas."

"Fine," said the Tinkerer, "but be quick. I haven't got all day. Do you think all this stuff just crafts itself?"

"Of course not," Bacca said.

He moved through the room to the table nearest to the Tinkerer. She watched him carefully through her many eyepieces. Bacca paused in front of the table and put his hand on his chin, lingering thoughtfully. He was doing his best play-acting, and hoped she didn't catch on.

"What can you tell me about this suit of diamond armor?" Bacca asked. "Do you think it would look good on me?"

"Ha!" scoffed the Tinkerer. "Shows how much you know. That's *horse* armor."

"Oh," said Bacca, pretending to blush. "My mistake."

"Yes," the Tinkerer continued. "I made it out of only the finest diamonds."

Bacca picked up the horse armor and examined it closely. It was easy to see that the diamonds were not fine at all, but brittle and jagged. If worn by a real horse, the diamonds in the armor would probably stab the beast—and probably the rider too. And they would definitely break on the first hit if ever tested in combat. Bacca said nothing, and put the armor back.

"Or what about this anvil?" Bacca asked. "Oof. It's so heavy, I can hardly pick it up. I'll bet I could use it to fix a lot of broken things, right?"

"That's right," said the Tinkerer. "One of my best creations. A finer anvil, you'll *never* find."

Except that every anvil Bacca had ever seen was better than this one. The anvil was made of iron blocks that looked intentionally misshapen, and of iron ingots that were cracked and incomplete. This anvil wouldn't work at all. Anything you put across it and tried to hammer back into shape was just going to end up worse than before. On top of that, the anvil looked ready to fall over. Bacca could imagine it tipping over and crushing a crafter's foot.

"A fine anvil," Bacca said. "Very fine. Tell me, are all the items in your workshop of such high quality?"

"Absolutely!" the Tinkerer snapped. "Why do you think I get so many supplicants?"

Bacca nodded as though he believed her. In truth, he was very confused. Why was this person so confused about her creations? More importantly, what did these horrible items have to do with the riddle? What did the creepers want him to do?

As Bacca looked across the inventory of strange, sad, and dangerous items in the workshop, a plan began to formulate in his mind. Maybe the crafter did not see what she was doing—in every sense of the word. Maybe the many tubes through which she looked didn't make things clearer at all, but instead made them worse. The more Bacca thought about it, the more it made sense.

"Hmm," Bacca sighed, pretending to be an indecisive customer who couldn't quite find anything he liked. "I don't know. There's a lot of great stuff here . . . but nothing that's absolutely what I had in mind. Do you do custom orders?"

"A *custom* order?" the Tinkerer said, her tools clacking together in excitement. "I do . . . but it'll cost you."

"Do you accept gold and diamonds?" Bacca said, giving her just a glimpse into his well-stocked inventory.

"Oh yes," the Tinkerer said greedily. "That will do nicely. Just tell me, what do you want crafted?"

"I warn you, what I have in mind is a bit *unusual*," Bacca said.

"I'll be able to do it," the Tinkerer responded quickly, obviously thinking about the money she would make.

"Okay then," Bacca said. "Because what I'd *really* like is a golden sword that deals two hearts of damage."

"No problem!" the Tinkerer said brightly. "I could craft that in my sleep."

"I wasn't finished," Bacca interjected. "I want a golden sword that does two hearts of damage . . . to the person who swings it."

The Tinkerer was confused and momentarily speechless. She cocked her head to the side to make sure she was hearing him right.

"You know," Bacca continued. "Maybe the handle of the sword could be crooked and pointy, so it would cut your hands when you swung it. And the blade would be uneven and heavy at the point, so you'd always be falling and injuring yourself whenever you tried to give a good whack."

Bacca was aware that there were already several swords in the Tinkerer's workshop that fit this description to a T.

"But . . . but . . ." the Tinkered began. "Why would you . . . ?"

"Oh, if you're not up to the challenge, don't worry," Bacca said. "I'm sure there's somebody around here who could craft me a golden sword like that. I've heard that down in the maze there's a crafting bat called the Wizard. I'll bet *he* could do it."

"I'm ten times better at crafting than that so-called Wizard!" snapped the Tinkerer, springing into action. "You want a sword that's going to hurt you every time you swing it? Fine! I'll make it for you!"

"Thank you so much," Bacca said. "And as part of my payment, I'll be happy to supply the materials."

Bacca reached into his inventory and took out two gold ingots. They were ideally formed, perfectly smooth, and they gleamed in the sunbeams that shone through the skylight above. He held them out to the Tinkerer.

Bacca was secretly nervous. Her reaction would determine whether or not his suspicion about the Tinkerer was right.

"Ahh," the Tinkerer said. "*Those* will do nicely. If you want a golden sword that's going to hurt its user, then you need corrupted, tarnished, uneven gold. In other words, gold *just like this*!"

Bacca knew the ingots were absolutely flawless in every way.

"Oh, and I suppose you'll also be needing a stick," Bacca said. He fished into his inventory and pulled one out. Bacca's sticks were among the finest in all the Overworld. They were straight and true in every way.

"That will also do nicely," said the Tinkerer, peering at the stick through several of her eyepieces. "Crooked and irregular . . . this will make a truly evil, malformed sword."

The Tinkerer accepted the stick and took it over to her crafting table.

"Is it okay if I watch?" Bacca asked deceptively. "I'm so curious to see how crafting is done."

"Fine," barked the Tinkerer. "Just don't get in the way."

"Of course not," Bacca said with a smile. "I wouldn't dream of it."

As Bacca looked on, the Tinkerer began to create the golden sword. She combined the gold ingots with the stick, and began forging an impressive blade with blow after blow of her crafting hammer. Periodically, she would stop and examine her progress through the different eyepieces. Then she would go back to hammering. The sword that began to take shape was absolutely stunning. It had a blade that was long and sharp and straight. The tip came to an impressive point, and the handle looked like it would provide an excellent grip. Bacca was a master crafter, but he had crafted few golden swords equal to this one.

"Here," the Tinkerer said, carefully handing the finished product to Bacca—almost as though she were afraid of it. "One corrupted golden sword. Just promise me you won't let anyone else use it. I don't want people to get hurt!"

Bacca tried not to laugh. Her workshop was filled with items that would *only* hurt people.

He also felt excited, believing his hunch about the Tinkerer to be right. He decided that one more piece of evidence would prove it beyond a doubt.

Accepting the beautiful, perfectly-formed sword, Bacca gave the Tinkerer a handful of diamonds as payment.

"This sword is wonderful," Bacca said. "Just what I needed. If only I had a golden helmet to go with it."

"I could do that for you," the Tinkerer said, hungry for more diamonds.

"Could you?" Bacca asked. "That would be grand! But it would also be a *special* kind of helmet. Instead of protecting me from damage, I would want it to make me take extra damage!"

"What?" said the Tinkerer, puttering her hand to her chest in horror.

"If someone hits me for one heart of damage, this helmet should make me take two," Bacca explained. "You could make the insides all spiky, so they poked me every time I took a blow. Or make the brim sharp and liable to injure me. Or figure out your own way of doing it. The point is, if I'm wearing this thing, I need to be taking twice as much damage!"

The Tinkerer rolled her eyes.

"As they say, the customer is always right," she said to him, then mumbled, "Even if the customer is apparently crazy."

"I expect you'll need more corrupted gold ingots," Bacca said. "Here you go."

He handed her five of the most perfect ingots ever smelted.

"Yes," the Tinkerer said, examining them through her many eyepieces. "These are definitely corrupted. Okay, I'll make you the helmet now. But don't say I didn't warn you!"

The Tinkerer returned to her crafting table and began to hammer the gold. As Bacca watched, the Tinkerer formed a fine, gleaming golden helmet. It had a strong, powerful dome that looked impossible to crack. It was seamless and well-balanced. The interior of the helmet was crafted to fit exactly against the contours of the wearer's head. Bacca guessed that a person putting it on would feel as though they were wearing nothing at all.

"One golden helmet for wounding . . . the person stupid enough to wear it," the Tinkerer said, handing her finished product to Bacca. "And whatever you do, don't put it on in here. I'm not about to get sued. Let me tell you, the creeper legal system is a nightmare! So much red tape. Or, in their case, purple tape. Don't ask."

Bacca quickly put the golden helmet into his inventory and paid the Tinkerer with another handful of diamonds.

"Speaking of creepers," Bacca said, "how did such a skilled crafter as yourself come to live in a big scary creeper fortress? I'd think you could set up shop anywhere you liked in this biome."

"Despite what I just said about their legal system, the creepers have been very good to me," said the Tinkerer.

"They *have*?" asked Bacca. "I thought creepers were mostly known for being—pardon my frankness—a bunch of jerks."

"Oh, not the creepers," said the Tinkerer. "You must be thinking of something else. Why, when I set up shop here, they became my best customers. They were so supportive! They took great pains—and great expense—to help me to become a better crafter. They supplied me with all the wonderful equipment you see here."

"Does that equipment include those long metal tubes you look through?" Bacca asked.

"Yes, they're the greatest gift of all," the Tinkerer said. "They helped me really take my crafting to the next level. I use them for everything now."

"Yes, I see that," Bacca said. "May I take a look? I'm a very curious person."

The Tinkerer hesitated. The long metal tubes with their glistening gem lenses were clearly her most-prized possession.

"I promise to only look, and not touch," Bacca said. "Pleeeeese?"

"Fine," the Tinkerer said. "But no touching."

The Tinkerer took off her large round hat with the tubes hanging down from strings on the brim. She held it out so Bacca could take a closer look.

The tubular eyepieces seemed to have every kind of glistening gem that Bacca knew, and quite a few he hadn't seen before. Some of the longer tubes were curved so that they must have had a series of gems inside, reflecting the light all around in different ways. Bacca realized that all of the gems—*all* of them—were clearly enchanted with creeper magic.

"May I look through one of the tubes?" Bacca asked. "Just once?"

The Tinkerer hesitated again.

"I'll give you a diamond," Bacca said. "It'll be the easiest money you ever made."

The Tinkerer was tempted.

"Okay," she said. "But make it quick."

Bacca put his eye up to one of the strange metal tubes. Through it, the world looked blurry and distorted, but also something more. *Wrong.* It was that same sense of wrongness that had struck him when he first walked into the Tinkerer's workshop.

Bacca held up the flawless golden sword that The Tinkerer had made for him. Through the enchanted lenses of the eyepiece, it looked like something a monster might wield—and so broken and unbalanced that it would be dangerous to the user.

Bacca put away the golden sword and gave the Tinkerer back her hat, who returned it to her head. Then she held out her hand, ready to receive the diamond Bacca had promised.

"I'm going to give you a diamond," Bacca said, fishing around in his inventory for one. "But I'm also going to give you something even more valuable: some good advice."

"Oh?" said the Tinkerer as Bacca handed over a shiny diamond. "And what makes you think I need advice?"

"These creepers . . ." Bacca began. "I don't think they have your best interests in mind. If they're the ones making you see the world this way, then they have played a very mean trick on you."

"What?" said the Tinkerer. "How dare you say that? The creepers have been nothing but kind to me, and they're my best customers. They *love* the things I make. My creations are very popular."

"Yes," said Bacca. "Because creepers like to hurt people. And I hate to tell you, but that's what your items do. They hurt people. If you'd just take a look without using those tubes . . ."

"Feh," the Tinkerer replied, dismissing the idea. "These 'tubes,' as you call them, give me the ability to see the world like I never was able to before, and to craft things more perfectly than I ever could have dreamt."

Bacca walked over to where the Tinkerer had created a furnace out of blocks of cobblestone. Normally, this device would be used to allow a crafter to smelt. But this furnace—as Bacca could easily see from across the room—was set up in a way to splash molten ore everywhere and probably catch the person trying to use it on fire.

"What do you see here?" Bacca said.

"Why, that's one of my signature items—a top-of-the-line crafting furnace," said the Tinkerer. "That model's very popular with the creepers. They love to give them as gifts."

"I'm sure they do," Bacca said.

"What's that supposed to mean?" said the Tinkerer.

"You should try looking at the furnace without your eyepieces," Bacca recommended.

"What?" said the Tinkerer. "And why would I do that?"

"Just give it a try," Bacca said. "Unless you're *afraid . . .*"

"Afraid?" said the Tinkerer angrily. "I'll show you who's afraid!"

The Tinkerer took off her hat and looked at the furnace without using any of her eyepieces. She examined the item in silence for a very long time. Her expression said that something was not quite adding up.

"Now that I look more closely, there does seem to be a small error in that piece," she admitted. "That you for pointing it out, I suppose. Congratulations. You found the one mistake I ever made."

Bacca tried not to laugh out loud.

"And now take a look at this," Bacca said, holding up a bow which would send an arrow careening back into the person who shot it.

"Ehh," said the Tinkerer, as though something was amiss. "*You* did that. You must have! Why did you break that perfectly good bow? That's going on your tab."

"I didn't break it," Bacca said. "You made it that way. You made all of the things in your workshop this way. I don't think you did it because you're a bad person. I think you did it because when you look through those creeper tubes, it distorts everything. How long has it been since you used your own eyes to look at something you crafted? Years? Decades?"

"I've been here a very long time," said the Tinkerer. "It's hard to remember a time before I used them."

"I think you're a very gifted crafter," Bacca said gently. "I really do. You've got tremendous natural talent. You've just been held back by those awful creepers. They've corrupted your abilities. These tubes make you do the *opposite* of what you intend. I think if you went back to working without them, you could be truly great again!"

The Tinkerer thought about this while looking at all of the items on the tables in her workshop. For the first time, she was seeing them as Bacca had when he entered the workshop. She saw the wrongness and hurtfulness of them. She looked stunned. Bacca realized it must be a lot to take in all at once.

"Oh no," said the Tinkerer, putting her hand to her mouth in terror. "What have I done?"

"There, there," Bacca said comfortingly. "It wasn't your fault. You were tricked by those creepers. They're a very tricky bunch, as I'm finding out."

"I can't believe it," the Tinkerer said. "All this time—all these years—I was never really looking at what I was creating. All of these items . . . they'll have to be destroyed I suppose, so nobody gets hurt."

"You can worry about that another day," Bacca told her.

"I wish . . . I just wish . . ." said the Tinkerer, trailing off as she tried to articulate the thought. "I wish I could leave this place for a while. I need a break from crafting. A new career would be nice. One where I don't do anything that hurts people. Or anything much at all."

"Hmm," said Bacca, thinking. "Do you ever leave your crafting workshop?"

"It's been ages since I've stepped outside of this place. Years and years."

"I've got an idea," Bacca said. "Come with me."

So the Tinkerer took off her tool belts and put away all her crafting gear and followed Bacca as they walked back down the quartz staircase to the entrance to the workshop. Bacca opened the quartz door, and there they stood. There was nothing but the tunnel beyond—leading back to Gargantua—and the guardhouse with the guard standing stalwart inside it.

"Ahh," said the guard. "Nice to see you again. How did your riddle solving go?"

"I'm still working on it," Bacca said. "But I feel I'm getting close to the solution."

"Oh, that marvelous to hear," said the guard.

"Listen," Bacca told him. "When we were talking before, you said something about doing this job until somebody came to relieve you?"

"I'm afraid that's correct," the guard said with a frown.

"Does it have to be a creeper who relieves you?" Bacca asked.

"Does it have to be a creeper . . ." the guard repeated. "I never really thought about that. I don't suppose it has to be, no. But then, who in the wide world of Minecraft would want *this* job?"

"Guard, I want you to meet the Tinkerer," Bacca said. "She's looking for a new line of work. Preferably one where she does as little as possible."

"I don't mind saying that this would be perfect for her, then," the guard said, turning to the Tinkerer. "All you do is stand here. Gives you a lot of time to have some really interesting thoughts. And now and then you meet nice people to talk to, like this hairy fellow Bacca."

"That sounds like exactly what I should be doing," the Tinkerer said. "Can I try on the hat?"

The guard happily handed his tall hat over.

"Wow!" she said. "This is much more comfortable than my old hat. Tell me, how does it look?"

"Very good," Bacca said. "Fits you perfectly."

The Tinkerer seemed quite pleased with this turn of events, and took the guard's place in the guardhouse. The guard was overjoyed to be released, and gave them both big hugs.

The only one who was not feeling ecstatically happy . . . was Bacca, who began angrily pacing the floor around the little guardhouse, looking up in the dark nooks and crannies of the ceiling.

"Okay, creepers!" he cried out to the darkness. "I've solved your riddle. Do you have any more, or can I please have the Dragon Orb back now?"

The creepers looked down at Bacca from their secret hiding place. They did not believe that

Bacca could truly see them, but it did appear that his gaze lingered in their direction a little longer than it should have. For many of the creepers, this was deeply unnerving.

"He's done it!" one of the creepers said—putting into words what all of them were thinking. "He's solved the final riddle!"

"Yes," said another creeper. "But that's exactly what we *wanted* him to do, remember? Everything has gone swimmingly."

"It has?" said a slightly confused creeper. "I mean . . . yes it has!"

"*Of course* it has," snapped the previous creeper. "He's passed all of our tests, and solved all of our riddles. But now comes the *truly* difficult part. Now we have to tell him why he's *really* here."

A general murmur of excitement ran through the creepers as they remembered what their original plan had been.

Then a small creeper at the back of the bunch found the courage to ask: "But . . . what if he says no?"

"If he says no!?!?!" thundered one of the senior creepers. "He's not going to say no! And do you know why? Because we will *make* him say yes!"

The creeper began to laugh. It was a dark, sadistic, evil laugh. It went on for a very long time.

The junior creepers looked back and forth at one another and smiled nervously. Very few of them actually understood what was going to happen next.

Chapter Twelve

Bacca scanned the darkness above, looking for the creepers. He could tell they were there. He could smell them. After years in the field, you learned to recognize a whiff of creeper.

Suddenly, there was a rustling from one of the room's dark corners, and a motley crew of purple creepers began to emerge. When they walked, they stuck together in a tight bunch. Bacca worried what would happen if they all decided to explode at once. The sheer force of it might blow a hole in their fortress. This fact alone, that even though creepers were real jerks, they probably weren't big enough jerks to ruin their own home, made Bacca feel safe.

"That's close enough," he recommended as the creepers drew near.

"Very well," whispered one of the creepers.

"Why are you whispering?" Bacca said. "We're not trying to keep secrets here."

"I'm not whispering," the creeper said, just barely loud enough to be heard. "I'm screaming. And boy, is my throat going to be sore tomorrow."

"Very well," Bacca said, rolling his eyes and mimicking the creepers. "So was that the final riddle? Did I solve it?"

Bacca had a feeling that he had.

"Yes," the creeper said.

"So then hand over the Dragon Orb," Bacca said.

"First, answer me a question," the creeper said. "Why do you think we took the orb?"

Bacca considered it. The obvious answer was because creepers were jerks. If they were jerks to crafters and villagers, then they were probably jerks to dragons too.

"Why don't *you* tell *me*?" Bacca said instead, tired of playing creeper games.

"We took it because we needed a crafter," the creeper said, who obviously was more excited to brag about how clever their plans had been than they were with tying Bacca up in a guessing game. "We needed a crafter far superior to any in our own server plane. But how to get a crafter? That was our dilemma. Creepers cannot travel far or fast. Creepers cannot transport crafters. But dragons can."

"Oh my goodness!" Bacca said. "You *used* the dragons!"

The creepers all nodded shamelessly.

"We knew the dragons would do anything to get their orb back," the creeper said. "They would travel far and wide to find the greatest, bravest, most worthy crafter in the multiverse. Then they would bring him or her right to us. And as it turned out, that crafter was you."

"I know I should be flattered," Bacca said. "But instead I feel like chopping you all up with my diamond axe. I wonder why that is."

"Now, now," the creeper cautioned. "Don't be hasty. You haven't finished hearing us out."

"Well then, out with it!" Bacca snapped. "Why did you have the dragons bring me here? What do you want with a crafter?"

"This fortress . . ." the creeper began tentatively. "It's getting old. And full. So many creatures and people have come to live here. There's hardly room to move!"

"*Seriously?*" Bacca said sarcastically. "*That's* why you brought me here?"

"We want a new fortress," the creeper said. "Not just a new fortress. A bigger, better one. The best that's ever been built—in any biome, on any server plane, in any Overworld, anywhere! For this, we knew we would need the best crafter in existence. So we hatched our plan."

"First you used the dragons, and now you want to use me?" Bacca said. "What a bunch of jerks!"

"Watch your tongue, mister," the creeper said sternly. "You may be a master crafter, but that's *all* you are. We are still creepers, and you're still a guest in our house. We could explode you any time we felt like it."

Bacca decided he was about through talking to creepers.

"I solved all your riddles, so give me the Dragon Orb," Bacca said, growing angry. "Those were the rules."

"The *rules?*" the creeper said sarcastically. "Ha ha ha! The rules are what we *say* they are."

"Yeah," added another creeper. "And right now, we say that you're going to build us a brand new fortress. One that's twice as big as this one. So everyone will know how powerful and important we are!"

"You're a bunch of crazies, is what you are," Bacca said. "How about this instead: You give me the Dragon Orb—*right now*—and I won't smash your fortress apart and take it. And I also might let a few of you walk out of here in one piece."

"Ha!" one of the creepers laughed dramatically. "I'd like to see you try."

"Yeah," said another creeper. "That's never going to happen."

"I know," said a third, "and it would be a total waste of time because the Dragon Orb's not even here!"

There was a sudden awkwardness among the creeper ranks.

"Quiet, you dolt!" one ordered.

"Shhh!" said another.

"Stop talking right now!" shouted a third. "If we aren't careful, then he's going to find out that we hid it down in the Nether!"

". . ."

All of the creepers turned and looked at the creeper who had just spoken.

"*Darn it!*" the creeper said.

The cat was out of the bag.

"Thanks very much for the information," Bacca said with a smirk, wondering how the same creepers that had put together such challenging riddles could be so careless as to ruin their own master plan. "It's been fun solving your riddles, but I'm afraid I must be going."

"Wait!" one of the creepers cried. "Do you think we're stupid?"

Bacca looked right and left, wondering if this was a trick question.

"Well, you *did* just accidently tell me where you'd hidden the Dragon Orb," Bacca said. "But . . . go on."

"We're not stupid enough to leave the orb unguarded," the creeper said. "The Nether is dangerous, and we have a bunch of friends down there.

I don't know how it is on your home server plane, but here the Nether is a horrible realm of lava and darkness and many dangers."

"No, that sounds about right," Bacca said, remembering with a shiver his last encounter there.

"In that case, you know what I'm talking about," the creeper replied. "To venture there means great danger. Why risk it? Why risk it on behalf of a bunch of dragons you don't even know? Why not instead stay here, and use your crafting powers to help us create the greatest, most impressive fortress in the history of . . . *hey, where are you going*???"

"See you later!" Bacca called as he headed back through the quartz door and began bounding up the steps two at a time. When he arrived at the Tinkerer's workshop, it took Bacca only a few moments to stack some chairs and tables high enough to reach the skylight above. Then Bacca climbed to the top of the stack and jumped through.

The creepers had not moved from the bottom of the staircase.

"Well . . . that didn't go very well," one of them said.

"This is all *your* fault," said another. "Why'd you have to open your big mouth up and blab about the orb being in the Nether?"

"I'm not so sure this is a problem," said a senior creeper who had been one of the chief architects of the plan. "No, this may end up being the very best thing for us. When Bacca goes to the Nether and sees how impossible it is to get the orb from where we've hidden it, he'll come crawling back to us. He'll *beg* to build us a new fortress. And then when he's finished, will we give him the orb? *Of course not!* Once the dragons had what they wanted from us, we'd be toast! Evaporated! Disintegrated! No, we'll keep it, and then we'll make Bacca keep doing whatever we say . . . forever!"

The senior creeper began to laugh hysterically. The other creepers smiled nervously, but were secretly disturbed. Sure, they were kind of jerks, but even this seemed like it might be crossing the line. And making them more uneasy was a sound they began to hear above the laughter. The sound of very large wings. Several pairs of very large wings . . .

From the top of the creeper fortress nestled high in the clouds, Bacca leapt onto the back of the Diamond Dragon. A swarm of other dragons had joined it, each made of a different material. They all looked into Bacca's eyes with a hopeful longing.

"Do you have it?" asked the Diamond Dragon urgently. "Did you get the orb back for us?"

"Um . . . let's just say that I've got some good news, and some bad news," Bacca said. "The bad news is that your orb isn't inside the creeper fortress. It never was. The good news is now I know exactly where it is."

"Where?" asked the Diamond Dragon excitedly. All the other dragons crowding the sky hovered close, listening in.

"They've hidden it somewhere down in the Nether," Bacca said.

There was a collective groan from all of the dragons.

"Ahh, we feared they might put it down there," said the Diamond Dragon. "The Nether is one of the few places where dragons cannot go!"

"Well it's definitely a place that Baccas can go," Bacca said. "Been there several times. I wouldn't recommend long visits, but it's not without its charms."

"You're still going to help us?" said the Diamond Dragon. "That's wonderful. Thank you so much."

"Of course, I'm going to help," said Bacca. "And not just because I like helping dragons. Those creepers have done bad things to a whole bunch of people. They stole your orb just to lure me here. They tricked a crafter into wearing eyepieces that would make her craft horrible monstrosities. And . . . and . . . probably a bunch of other stuff we don't even know about yet! Anyhow, my point is, anything that upsets those creepers' plans just got moved to the top of my agenda."

"Glad to hear it," said the Diamond Dragon.

"Is there a Nether Portal around here?" Bacca asked.

"Yes, there is," the Diamond Dragon replied. "Not far from here is a forest with a great tree in the center. At the top of this tree you will find a Nether Portal. It is the only one we know of on this server plane. I can take you to it right now."

With Bacca clinging to its back, the Diamond Dragon swooped down from the top of the creeper fortress and flew far across the landscape until a lush green forest appeared on the horizon. The other dragons flew alongside. The expressions on their faces were ones of unhappiness and unease. Several of the dragons were orange, and maybe one of them might have been the Pumpkin Dragon— whom Bacca still *very* much wanted to meet—but this felt like the wrong time to try to make introductions. The dragons were clearly preoccupied.

"Psst, hey," Bacca said into the Diamond Dragon's ear. "Why is everybody in such a bad mood?"

"With every hour that passes without the Dragon Orb in our possession, we grow weaker," answered the Diamond Dragon. "Soon we may lose the power even to fly."

Looking around at the formation of dejected, nervous dragons made Bacca feel sad. He kicked himself for ever believing the creepers would be true to their word and return the orb if he solved the riddles. Creepers were jerks, that much he already knew, but now he knew they were also liars. Bacca was determined that no matter what challenge lay on the other side of the Nether Portal, he would do whatever it took to find the Dragon Orb and bring it back safely to the dragons.

The forest on the horizon drew near. At first, Bacca had wondered if it would be hard to locate the tallest tree. Then he saw a central one in the very middle of the forest that grew three times as wide and twice as tall as all of the others. Not even a creeper could have failed to spot it. And there at the very top, glistening like a holiday ornament, was a shining portal to the Nether.

The Diamond Dragon reached the great tree and began to circle it, flying ever higher with each rotation. Soon, it reached the toppermost branch and Bacca jumped off. The other dragons circled warily below. Bacca could still see the worried expressions on their faces.

Wasting no time, he lunged into the Nether Portal and felt himself pass through to the other side . . . where an entirely new reality awaited him.

Bacca took a deep breath, and quickly regretted it. The air around him was smoky and metallic.

Underneath his feet, a floor of dark netherrack seemed to extend endlessly in all directions. Interrupting the uniformity of the floor were long rivers of hissing, burbling lava. Patches of fire burned randomly across the dark, endless terrain.

Trips through Nether Portals were seldom pleasant, and this one had been no exception. Bacca had arrived face-first in a pile of gravel and soul sand. He stood up and brushed his suit off, then spit a few bits of gravel out of his mouth.

"Pfft!" Bacca said. "Stupid gravel. Okay. Time to find that Dragon Orb!"

He set off across the dark, mysterious landscape. He had no sense of where the orb might be found, but Bacca reminded himself that it had been taken here by creepers. They probably hadn't thrown it through the Nether Portal and called it a day. He knew he was looking for something which the creepers *didn't* want him to find. In Bacca's mind, this left two likely possibilities. The orb was probably either hidden in the darkest corner of the Nether where nobody would ever think to look . . . or put somewhere that nobody would dare to go.

Bacca scoured the ground all around him. Sooner rather than later, he found what he was looking for. Creeper tracks. Lots and lots of them.

"Only creepers could be this dumb," Bacca said to himself. "They think being quiet makes up for everything else. What a bunch of idiots. I'll bet this trail leads right to the Dragon Orb."

Aware that time was of the essence—the dragons growing weaker and weaker with every passing moment—Bacca took off across the dusty plain of netherrack in the direction of the creeper footprints.

He made good time until a group of ghasts floated into view. He could hear their pitiful moans from yards away. Ghasts were the saddest creatures that Bacca knew—even sadder than dragons who'd had their orb stolen. This group was floating right above the trail of creeper footprints, effectively blocking the way forward.

Bacca always liked to give potential foes the option to rethink their plans to attack him—partly because he was a nice guy, but also because fighting was just *so* much more work than negotiating—but before he had time to present a persuasive argument, the mewling, floating balls of tentacles began spitting searing balls of fire at him.

"Hey!" Bacca said, jumping out of the way. "Knock it off, or Betty and I are going to give you something to *actually* be sad about!"

Whoosh! Another fireball zoomed past. These ghasts were not going to listen to reason. Fine, thought Bacca, maybe they would listen to being hacked apart.

Bacca took Betty out of his inventory and jumped into the fray.

Whack! Whack! Whack!

One of the ghasts fell out of the air.

Whack! Whack! Whack!

A second one fell.

The ghasts seemed to sense that they had bitten off more than they could chew. They began drifting up toward the dark ceiling of the Nether.

"Oh no you don't," Bacca said, taking out a bow enchanted with Power and Infinity arrows.

Zip! Zip! Zip!

Bacca's arrows flew through the air, and the ghasts began to fall one after the other. Soon it devolved into an all-out ghast retreat. The mournful balls of tentacles high-tailed it in all directions.

"See?" Bacca said. "That's what you get when you spit fireballs at people for no reason."

He tried to think of other insults to shout at the ghasts, but stopped when he saw what they had been blocking.

The terrain behind the ghasts was a very strange sight. Three different rivers of lava joined, forming a great circle and creating a single island with a lava moat around it. The island rose up into the air—not quite a mountain, but at least a very large hill. And all across this hill, strange figures moved in the darkness. The glow of the lava cast strange, spooky shadows across them.

As he edged closer, Bacca realized that what he was seeing was not a trick of perspective. Some of the figures on the hill were the same size as Bacca . . . but others were enormous. As big as Gargantua had been. Giants. Real giants. They had to be. Perhaps this was what Gargantua had once been, before he became a skeleton. They stumbled around ponderously, making huge *THUD!* sounds with their feet. They frowned and had huge, bushy eyebrows. They did *not* look friendly.

The other, smaller, figures were not as aggressive. They also looked familiar. Bacca realized he had seen one of their kind quite recently. They were iron golems. There had to be hundreds of them walking around the hill beneath the giants. The two species seemed to coexist there, like animals that shared the same space but never seemed to notice one another.

Then something important caught Bacca's attention. At the very top of the hill was a pedestal made of diorite blocks. And on the pedestal was a cloth made of woven gold ingots. And on the cloth was a large glowing orb that changed color as Bacca watched it, gradually cycling through the entire rainbow. And on the side of the orb was a giant letter "D."

"And here I thought it would be an uppercase D . . ." Bacca said to himself.

This had to be the Dragon Orb, he thought. The creepers had chosen to hide it in plain sight . . . in a place where very few people would be brave enough to go.

Bacca walked closer, and as he neared the edge of the river of lava, the giants began to notice him. Their faces got even frownier. Bacca didn't know what they were going to do, but it didn't look like they wanted to be friends.

He tried to think up a plan for reaching the orb. The first challenge, he realized, would be the ring of lava. Most of the time, lava ran in thin streams that were easy to jump. But this river was as thick as ten or fifteen of those combined. Jumping was not going to be an option.

"I'll have to build a bridge," Bacca said to himself. "Good thing there's plenty of crafting material down here to work with."

But no sooner were these words out of his mouth than an enormous wave of lava lapped against the side of the moat. It sent the fiery red ore hundreds of feet into the air.

"Yikes," Bacca said. "What was *that* about?"

Bacca decided to wait and watch the lava flow. Before long another great lava wave lapped up against the land. And then another.

Bacca realized that these jets of lava were going to crash up into the air at regular intervals. Any crafting blocks in the path of their spray would probably be done for, quickly disintegrated by the intense heat. As would any crafters. Building a bridge over this lava was something that would have to be done *very* quickly.

Bacca's train of thought was derailed as suddenly a giant boulder smacked into the side of his head. He took two hearts of damage and was knocked onto his back. He looked up to see that the giants had started throwing boulders at him. One of them did a wind-up like a baseball pitcher and hucked its boulder as hard as it could. Bacca rolled out of the way just in time to avoid being hit.

"It looks like talking things out with these guys is off the table," Bacca said, reaching for his bow. "And if I have to take them out, I guess it should be sooner rather than later."

Bacca nocked an arrow and began to fire across the lava moat at the giants. The giants, in turn, continued to throw their boulders in his direction. He had never faced giants before and did not know what to expect from them in battle. It turned out that their boulders were easy to dodge. It was also not very hard to hit them with arrows. They moved slowly and were difficult to miss. The problem, Bacca soon realized, was their health. They had lots and lots *and lots* of it. Bacca's arrows were straight and deadly, but the giants took all the damage he could dish out without much effect.

How many hearts of health did these creatures have? Hundreds? Thousands?

Finally, Bacca hit one of the giants enough times that it began to teeter. He grew excited. Maybe one of them would actually go down. But then his heart sank!

From out of its inventory, Bacca watched the wounded giant pull an enormous healing potion. The giant drank it down. Moments later, it roared back into the fight looking completely restored.

Bacca suddenly had a feeling that this approach wasn't going to work. Even if he shot arrows at them for days, who knew how long it would take to defeat these giants. And if they were going to be using healing potions on top of it? Why, it could take weeks. Or months!

Bacca didn't think the dragons had that kind of time.

Finally, he considered that even when he *did* defeat the giants, there would be the matter of the golems. There were hundreds of them still standing between him and the Dragon Orb. How long would it take to defeat all of *them*?

As he continued to dodge boulders, Bacca pondered over the best approach.

Getting the orb from this island was going to be a tough job. There was no doubt about it. But Bacca began to suspect that the task just might be possible . . . with a little help from some of his new friends.

CHAPTER THIRTEEN

The dragons eyed the Nether Portal, waiting anxiously for Bacca to return. The absence of the Dragon Orb continued to affect them. Most were now too weak to fly, and sat on branches, their necks craned hopefully toward the top of the tree.

Suddenly, there was a great flash accompanied by a sound like thunder, and Bacca emerged from the portal. The dragons looked anxiously for any clue that his mission had been successful.

The Diamond Dragon hovered near the portal, smiling hopefully.

"Do you have it?" asked the dragon.

"Not yet," said Bacca. "But I'll have it soon. I just need a little help."

"I fear we are now too weak to be much help," the Diamond Dragon said. "Few of us can fly. And we cannot go into the Nether."

"If there are three dragons that still can fly, then my plan will work!" Bacca said confidently.

"I'm weakened . . . but you can still count on me," said the Diamond Dragon.

"And me," said the Emerald Dragon, swooping into view.

"And me too," said the Gold Dragon, taking flight from a nearby branch.

"Great," said Bacca. "Now here's what I need you to do."

Bacca whispered his instruction into each of the dragon's ears.

"What?" said the Emerald Dragon. "What good will *that* do?"

"Yeah," said the Gold Dragon. "I don't understand."

The Diamond Dragon came to Bacca's defense.

"Listen, you two," said the giant, glistening creature. "Since he arrived, Bacca has done everything he could to help us. He's risked life and limb—and probably lots of other stuff too—in order to find our orb. I may not entirely understand Bacca's plan, but something tells me he's earned our trust!"

A chorus arose from the other dragons on the branches.

"Yes!" they shouted. "He has earned our trust! Follow his plan!"

The emerald and gold dragons relented.

"Very well," said the Emerald Dragon. "We may not understand it, but we will follow his plan." He then flew in close to Bacca and looked at him with an enormous eye. "But this had better work!"

"Don't worry about that," Bacca told him. "You just do your part, and we'll have your orb back in no time."

"Let's get going," the Diamond Dragon said. "We weaken with every passing second. There's not a moment to lose."

The Emerald Dragon and the Gold Dragon flew off in different directions. Bacca jumped aboard the back of the Diamond Dragon, and then they too flew off across the treetops.

Leaving the forest behind, they crossed new landscapes that changed several times. Soon the creeper fortress towered into view.

The Diamond Dragon swiftly climbed up, up, up to the highest reaches of the great black obelisk, until it found the skylight through which Bacca had exited earlier.

"Right here?" asked the Diamond Dragon.

"Yes, this is perfect," he said, leaping from the beast's glistening back.

Bacca went back through the skylight and lowered himself into the workshop of the Tinkerer. Once there, he began to gather items from the workshop's tables and bring them back outside . . . where he placed them on the back of the diamond dragon. Bacca was a fast worker, and soon the dragon's back had a large mound of items spread across it. When it flew, Bacca suspected the dragon was going to look like a floating garage sale.

"Okay," said Bacca. "That's the last of them. I'll meet you back at the Nether Portal."

"Yes," said the Diamond Dragon. "I understand."

The dragon took off and headed back toward the forest. Bacca watched it fly away and decided he was right. The dragon *did* look an awful lot like a floating garage sale.

The sky above began to darken.

"Perfect," Bacca said. He jumped back through the skylight and closed it behind him.

Racing through the Tinkerer's workshop, Bacca hurdled across crafting tables and jumped over chairs on his way to the staircase. He raced down the steps and passed through the quartz door.

There, he saw the guard house with the Tinkerer still standing at attention inside it.

"Hello," she called in a delighted voice. "Oh, Bacca! I wasn't expecting to see you again so soon. I have to thank you again—I absolutely love my new job as a guard. It really gives me a lot of time to myself."

"That's great," said Bacca, racing past. "Sorry, I don't have time to talk right now. I'll see you later!"

And Bacca sprinted past her down the corridor to the small ledge overlooking the mammoth room where Gargantua lived. The three enormous, toppled statues were still there—with giant arrows still embedded in them—but the villagers had entirely removed the golden sun from the wall. (Bacca hoped they had acted really frightened when they gave all the gold back to the ghost.)

"Hello!" said an enormous voice. "What Are You Doing Back Here?"

"I have some exciting news," Bacca told Gargantua. "I know that you really enjoyed our little skeleton simulation. But what if I told you that I've found a way you could hunt people your own size . . . for real!"

"I Would Do Anything To Make That Happen," Gargantua said excitedly.

"In that case, pick me up from this ledge," Bacca said. "We'll need to work quickly."

A giant skeletal hand shot through the gloom and hovered next to Bacca, who climbed aboard. Gargantua lifted him up to his enormous bony face. Bacca could see the giant skeleton's newfound excitement written all over his face. Err . . . skull.

"Now that I've made my way through it, I have a better sense of the dimension of this fortress," said Bacca. "I used to think this room was far underground, but now I realize it's about ground level. And by my calculation, the external wall of the fortress is *that* wall there."

Bacca gestured to the far side of the room.

"By Where I Shot The Villagers You Made . . . The Ones That Were *My* Size?"

"Yes, exactly," Bacca said. "Now unfortunately, I don't have time to carve a door that's big enough for you. But I think if you can hold me up, I'll be able to carve the outline of a door. Then you should be able to push your way through."

"Good," said the giant. "Let Us Begin. I Am Quite Excited By This Plan."

Gargantua's enthusiasm made Bacca laugh. He took his favorite diamond pickaxe out of his inventory and took a few practice swings.

"Okay," Bacca said. "What I need you to do is pretend that I'm a pencil you're holding. I want you to use me to draw a door on the wall—one that will be big enough for you to fit through."

"Yes," boomed the giant. "I Can Do That."

"But don't actually try to draw with me," Bacca cautioned. "Because you'll smush me if you do that. Instead, just hold me up to the wall."

"I Understand," the giant said.

Bacca sincerely hoped he did.

Starting at the ground level where the wall met the floor of the room, Gargantua slowly began to use Bacca to draw the shape of an enormous door. Bacca swung his pickaxe wildly, faster than he ever had before, and crushed through the blocks in front of him. Whenever a block was demolished, the giant moved him a little higher, giving him access to the next block.

As he worked away, Bacca was relieved to see that he had been right about the position of the room. It was directly against the fortress's outer wall. Not only that, but the wall was quite thin. As Bacca chopped away blocks, he found he could see moonlight streaming in from outside.

"Keep up the good work," Bacca cried to the giant. "We're getting there!"

More quickly than Bacca anticipated, they were able to trace the outline of a huge door into the side of the castle wall. Bacca had never smashed blocks so quickly in all of his life. His shoulder hurt and his fingers were starting to get blisters. His once-sharp diamond pickaxe now looked blunt and dull. He just hoped that his efforts would be enough to free Gargantua.

"Okay," Bacca said as the giant deposited him back on the floor. "Now I need you to get a running start and put your shoulder into that door we've made. Or your shoulder bone. Whatever."

"Yes," said Gargantua. "I Will Do It."

The giant took a few thundering steps back-wards, then ran full-tilt into the outline of the door. There was a sound like a cannon being fired as Gargantua collided into the wall. Then, very slowly, the piece of wall began to fall forward. Anticipating another loud noise, Bacca put his fingers in his ears as he watched it fall.

KER-CHUNK!!!

The great mass of blocks hit the ground with a force that made the earth shake. After the dust had cleared, Bacca and Gargantua found themselves staring out into the darkened biome beyond. The moon was high in the sky.

"This World Beyond . . . It Looks So Strange," said the giant, peering out nervously.

"Now's not the time to be timid!" Bacca cried. "We've still got important work to do. Pick me up and put me on your shoulder."

The giant did so.

"Good," Bacca said. "Now, do you know what 'running' is? Because I'm going to need you to run as fast as you can all the way to the forest. Don't worry about directions. I'll let you know where to turn."

"Running?" the Giant said. "Yes, I Have Heard Of This. But My Confines Were Always Too Small To Attempt It."

"Well let's try it right now," Bacca said. "There's never a better time than the present!"

Gargantua turned out to be an excellent runner. Like a horse, he was slow getting started, but really flew along once he got up to top speed. With Bacca shouting directions into his ear, the enormous skeleton ran in the direction of the forest.

Soon, the green leaves and brown branches of the trees came into view. Bacca saw that the Diamond Dragon was already waiting for him on the highest branch of the tallest tree. The Emerald Dragon was there too . . . and he had brought along another familiar face.

Gargantua jogged closer, knocking over or entirely trampling smaller trees as he did so. The multitude of dragons who were too sickly to fly looked on in amazement as the biggest skeleton they had ever seen came running up.

"Whoa there," Bacca cried. "Stop right in front of that tall tree with the glistening portal on top."

Gargantua obeyed. The skeleton was so tall that his head was more or less level with the Nether

Portal at the top of the tree. Bacca jumped onto the nearest branch and eyed the Emerald Dragon. And an iron golem sitting next to him.

"You wouldn't *believe* how hard it was to convince him to do this!" the Emerald Dragon said to Bacca. "I had to do everything but threaten him!"

"Hello, Bill!" Bacca said. "Thank you for coming."

"I didn't really have a choice," the iron golem said. "When a dragon 'strongly suggests' you do something, they can be surprisingly convincing."

"I know the feeling," Bacca said.

"The Emerald Dragon said if I helped you, then you would show me the best place of all to be a hermit," Bill related. "Is this true? You know of a place better than the ice wastes?"

"Indeed I do," said Bacca. "And it's just through that glowing doorway there."

Bill looked doubtfully at the Nether Portal.

"We're just waiting on the Gold Dragon, who will be bringing our final team member," Bacca said. "He should be here any—"

No sooner were these words out of Bacca's mouth than the outline of the Gold Dragon loomed into view on the horizon. Bacca smiled. Then his jaw dropped a little in surprise, as instead of carrying one person on its back . . . there were two.

The Gold Dragon circled once and then landed next to Bacca. On its back sat the Wizard, now in his human form. But sitting next to him was a witch, the very same one who had imprisoned and cursed the Wizard! Looking more closely, Bacca realized both of them were wearing gold rings . . . and they were holding hands!

"Hi Bacca," both of them said at once.

"You *got married*!?" Bacca asked in amazement.

"Well, you know how it goes," the Wizard said sheepishly. "We started talking, and found out we really had a lot in common. Crafting items and brewing potions really aren't that different if you stop and think about it."

"Yes, and I'm totally sorry I ever turned him into a bat," added the witch. "What a mistake! But that's in the distant past now, isn't it dear?"

"Of course it is," said the Wizard, giving her a smooch on the cheek.

Bacca had seen many strange things during this adventure, but someone kissing a witch had to be the strangest so far.

"When the dragon said you needed help, I said 'Just tell me where and when,'" continued the Wizard.

"And I insisted on coming," added the witch. "We go everywhere together now."

"Okay," Bacca said to the witch, happy to have an extra pair of hands. "I'm sure you can find a way to help. The more the merrier!"

"So what's all this about?" the Wizard asked. "Why did you bring us here?"

"Yeah," said the witch.

"Yeah," said Bill the iron golem.

"Yeah," said Gargantua.

Bacca smiled.

"There's a challenge on the other side of that Nether Portal standing between me and the Dragon Orb," he explained. "I've got to get it back or these dragons will keep getting sicker. This is not a challenge I can complete on my own . . . but I think I can do it with your help."

"We have to go with you through the portal?" asked the Wizard. "Sounds like an adventure!"

"Ooh, I've never been to the Nether," said the witch. "I wonder if it's a good place for a honeymoon."

"I'll Never Fit Through That Tiny Door," said Gargantua. He looked at the ground sadly. Bacca worried that the giant felt left out because he was differently sized.

"Don't worry," Bacca said to the giant skeleton. "A Nether Portal isn't like a regular door. Just touch it with your finger, and you'll be teleported to the other side."

"Oh Good," said Gargantua, brightening. "I Can Do That!"

"Now, let's not waste any more time standing around talking," Bacca said. "With each minute that passes, these poor dragons get weaker. They need their orb, and we're going to get it for them! I just need you all to do *one* last thing before we leave."

"What's that?" asked the Wizard.

"You may have noticed that the Diamond Dragon is covered in a bunch of strange items and looks like a garage sale," Bacca said. "Before you go through the portal, I need each one of you to fill your inventories with as many of these items as you can carry. Do not—I repeat—*do not* try to use any of them. Just carry them for now. Here, I'll go first."

Bacca leapt beside the Diamond Dragon. He emptied his inventory of everything non-essential for this trip. (That meant only Betty, his diamond pickaxe, and a suit of diamond armor would go along for the ride.) Then Bacca took as many of the strange items as he could carry from the collection draped across the Diamond Dragon.

The Wizard, the witch, Bill, and even Gargantua all followed Bacca's example and filled their inventories until they were practically bursting.

"Ahh, that's better," the Diamond Dragon said. "I was feeling a little squished under all that!"

"Okay," Bacca said. "It's time to go to the final test. I'm confident we can do this. We know where the Dragon Orb is, and now we have the tools to get it. Come on everybody!"

And with that he leapt through the portal and into the Nether.

chapteq fouqteen

Thud.
Thud.
Thud.
Thud.

There were four sounds of human-sized things landing on the gravelly floor of the Nether. Bacca, the Wizard, the witch, and Bill all stood up and dusted themselves off.

"Um, guys . . . I think we all ought to get out of the way," Bacca said.

The group hurried to the side as a great bony shape fell out of the darkness above.

THUD!!!

"You Were Right, Bacca," the giant said, righting itself. "I Only Had To Touch It With My Finger. So This Is The Nether? Hmmm. It's Nice And Dark. Kind Of Reminds Me Of Home. Only With A Lot More Room To Move Around."

The group followed Bacca as he retraced the path of the creepers across the netherrack floor. Several mobs of ghasts hovered nearby. Perhaps remembering their disastrous battle with Bacca (or maybe noticing the biggest skeleton they had ever seen behind him), they chose not to attack.

As always, the Nether was oppressive and hot and smelly. The witch turned up her nose.

"Nope," she said. "Definitely not a good place for a honeymoon."

"Ahh, but a fine place for a hermit," Bill said. "People would really leave me alone if I was down here."

"Just wait," Bacca said. "You ain't seen nothing yet."

Bacca and his party crossed the bleak Netherscape until the moat of lava came into view, and then the hill beyond it. At its peak, the Dragon Orb let off its steady, multicolored glow. Now and then, splashes of lava leapt into the sky.

It was very dramatic.

"*That's* where we're going?" asked Bill. "It doesn't look very nice at all."

"Trust me," Bacca said. "It's going to be great."

Soon the giants who inhabited the island noticed that they had some new visitors. Bacca could tell by the position of their hairy, expressive eyebrows that they were nervous about his new friends. Or, more specifically, about Gargantua.

Bacca glanced up over his shoulder at the giant skeleton. He wondered if Gargantua would require any prompting. As it turned out, the answer was no.

"I Am Having The Strangest Feelings Just Now," the huge skeleton announced.

"Oh really?" Bacca said. "Tell me about them."

"I Have The Urge To Pull Out My Bow And *SHOOT SHOOT SHOOT* At Those Giants Until They Are No More," Gargantua said. "The Impulse Is Almost Uncontrollable."

"Good," Bacca said with a smile. "Because that's why you're here. I say if it feels good, do it!"

"I Will!" proclaimed the giant, rushing forward. "I Will!"

As Bacca and the others looked on, Gargantua sprinted to the edge of the moat of lava. The giants on the island seemed to sense what was about to happen, because they were already picking up boulders to throw. Gargantua raised his huge bow and nocked an arrow. He pulled back on the string and let it fly. The arrow arced across the river of lava and struck one of the giants in the middle of the chest. It took several hundred hearts of damage and toppled over.

"Ahh, now I see why you brought *him!*" the Wizard said as they watched Gargantua firing away.

"Yeah," Bacca answered. "I tried shooting those giants myself, but there was just no way to do enough damage. I think Gargantua solves that problem rather nicely."

"And it comes to him naturally, by the looks of it," observed the Wizard.

"Well, he is a skeleton after all," Bacca said. "Just a very big one."

The battle continued. Now and then one of the giants managed to land a boulder on Gargantua, but it was usually a glancing blow. Gargantua, on the other hand, turned out to have excellent aim. Almost all of his arrows were right on target.

"Wow!" added the Wizard. "He was born to do it. Or reanimated to do it. Whatever skeletons are."

Bacca nodded in agreement.

After only a few minutes of firing, the giant population on the island had been completely decimated. Gargantua's bony eye sockets scanned for any sign of further giant activity. Detecting none, the skeleton reluctantly lowered his bow.

"Nice work!" Bacca said.

"Yes," agreed Gargantua. "That Was Very Satis-fying Indeed."

"Okay," Bacca said, turning to the Wizard. "This is where I'm going to need *your* help. To get to the island, we're going to have to craft a bridge over the lava and run across."

"Hmm, that shouldn't be too much of a chal-lenge," said the Wizard. "Why did you need me for that?"

"Watch how the lava splashes up, every few moments," Bacca said. "See that?"

As Bacca spoke those words, a huge wave of lava washed up right next to where they were standing. The air was filled with a hot burning stench. They all took a step back to avoid being sprayed.

"I do!" said the Wizard. "I *do* see that."

"Right," Bacca continued. "So we're going to have to build this bridge *very quickly*—between lava splashes. We'll have to mine some netherrack and smelt it into nether bricks, but that shouldn't take long at all. Then we'll use the nether bricks to build a bridge. Nether brick is resistant to fire, but if you start a fire on a block of nether brick it will burn forever. So if the lava splashes up before we're done, two things could happen—and they're both bad. One, it might wash away the bridge and we fall into the lava. Or two, it might only set the whole bridge on fire and burn us up."

"Yikes," the Wizard said, looking afraid. "Those are both bad options."

"But don't worry," Bacca said. "With two crafters working together, I'm sure we can build the bridge in time. Well . . . *reasonably* sure."

Suddenly, Bill interjected.

"I've got an idea," the iron golem said. "Why don't you just have Gargantua lie down over the lava and walk across his back? He's easily taller than the lava is wide!"

"I thought about that," said Bacca. "It won't work for a number of reasons. Gargantua isn't as solid as a bridge. We might fall through his ribs or slip on his vertebrae and go tumbling into the lava. Bones aren't really made to be walked on. Also, he would almost definitely get splashed by the lava and die, and I can't ask him to make that sacrifice for us. But finally—and most importantly—Gargantua wouldn't agree to do it! At their core, skeletons are very selfish. Even nice ones."

"This Is True," boomed Gargantua. "I Only Came To Shoot Giants."

"Then it's settled," said the Wizard. "Building a bridge is the only way. I'll start mining the netherrack to make us some nether bricks."

"Can I do anything to help?" asked the witch.

"Yes," Bacca said. "I know you specialize in offensive potions that make people take damage—on account of your being a witch and all—but how about crafting us some powerful potions of swiftness and potions of leaping? If we drink potions of swiftness, we'll be able to craft the bridge and run across it much more quickly."

"I see," said the witch. "And the potions of leaping?"

"If we don't get the bridge entirely finished, and we see a lava wave coming . . . we might have to jump the rest of the way," Bacca said.

The team got to work. Bacca and the Wizard began creating nether bricks, and the witch brewed powerful potions for every member of their group.

"What am I supposed to do?" asked Bill.

"See those hundreds and hundreds of golems who are still on the island?" Bacca asked.

"Yes I do, and it concerns me," Bill said. "They're all going to see me, which is really bad for a hermit. Plus, they don't look particularly friendly!"

"Well just hang tight," Bacca said reassuringly. "Once we get across the lava, you're going to help us with them. You'll have the most important job of all."

"Uh oh," said Bill. "I've got a bad feeling about this."

Bacca and the Wizard soon had more than enough bricks for the job.

"Here you go," the witch said, passing out her potions to everyone. "Bottoms up!"

The group drank down the potions.

"Okay, fellow crafter," Bacca said to the Wizard. "Let's do this!"

Bacca and the Wizard waited for the lava to splash in front of them. When it did, they started crafting a bridge like crazy. Bacca was instantly glad he hadn't tried to do this by himself. Even with the potion of swiftness coursing through his veins, he realized it would have been very tough for him to complete the bridge alone before the next lava splash. But with the Wizard working alongside him, it looked like they just might do it!

Soon they were halfway across the river of lava.

"No turning back now!" Bacca said to the Wizard.

"Aye aye!" the Wizard replied.

They continued building the bridge as quickly as they could. Soon they were three quarters of the way across.

Then it happened.

The lava beneath them began to swell. Bacca realized a new wave was building, and the bridge would position them right above it. It was time to make a tough decision.

"Okay!" Bacca called. "Everyone over the bridge now. The lava's about to erupt again. We'll have to jump the rest of the way!"

Bill, the witch, and the enormous skeleton scrambled onto the simple, no-frills bridge of nether brick that Bacca and the Wizard had constructed.

"Okay," Bacca said. "Here we go. All together. One . . . Two . . . *Three!*"

They leapt from the edge of the bridge across the river of lava. Boosted by their potions of leaping, each one of them made it safely to the shore on the other side. Instants later, a wave of lava crashed over the three-quarters completed bridge. It did not wash away, but every part of the bridge was now on fire.

"Whew!" Bacca said. "Everybody okay?"

The group dusted themselves off and did a quick inspection. Everyone had made it intact.

"Are we going to have to do that again to get *off* the island?" asked the Wizard.

"Probably," said Bacca. "But don't worry. If we did it once, we can totally do it again!"

"Uh . . . guys?" the witch said ominously. She was tapping Bacca and the Wizard insistently on the shoulders.

"What is it, my dear?" the Wizard said, turning around.

"What are we supposed to do about *them*?" said the witch.

Bacca and the Wizard saw hundreds of iron golems marching in their direction.

"Why do they look so angry?" asked the Wizard.

"Most golems defend villages, or they defend the people who created them," said Bacca. "I'm going to bet these golems were created by The Creep. And The Creep told the golems that this island was their village."

This was confirmed instants later when the golems got a few steps closer and began shouting at Bacca's group.

"You guys are in big trouble!" said one of the golems.

"The creepers told us that bad people might come here and try to take the orb," said another. "We are sworn to protect it!"

"You may have beat up the giants, but you won't be able to beat up all of us!" said another.

Bacca knew that the golem was right. He had always known it. There were simply too many to fight. Even with Betty freshly sharpened and a team of four friends, Bacca reckoned his chances against so many enemies in combat was not good. (The witch could certainly fight—Bacca knew that better than anybody—but the Wizard was a crafter not a fighter. Bill was likewise unproven in combat. And Bacca knew that giant skeletons were less effective against hordes than you might think. Even with enormous arrows, they could only shoot one target at a time. They might step on some of the enemy too, but that would most likely happen by accident.) This was why Bacca had formulated a different approach entirely.

"Okay," Bacca said to Bill. "Here's what I need you to do."

Bacca quickly whispered his instructions into the iron golem's ear.

"*Really?*" said Bill. "You want me to do *that?*"
Bacca nodded.

"But I'm a hermit!" Bill said. "Public speaking is like *my worst fear.*"

"I need you to trust me," Bacca said. "Everything's going to be okay. Do you trust me?"

"I guess so," answered Bill sheepishly.

"Okay then," Bacca said. "Then the rest is up to you."

While the rest of the group—including Bacca—looked on, Bill raised his iron golem arms above his head and addressed the angry horde marching toward them. Bacca was nervous. From this point on, their success or failure would all depend on Bill's talent . . . as an actor.

"My fellow golems!" shouted Bill at the top of his lungs. "We're not here to fight you! We're here to give you a bunch of cool stuff."

The golems were close enough that they could have lashed out and started the battle if they'd wanted to. Instead, they hesitated. This was an potentially intriguing proposal.

"Keep going, Bill," Bacca urged.

"That's right," said Bill. "We brought you presents. The creepers said we should bring them. I'm a fellow golem, so you can trust me on this."

The golems looked at one another, suspicious and confused.

"If you guys are with the creepers . . . then how come your big skeleton shot all our giants?" one of the golems asked.

"Because . . ." Bill said. "Um . . ."

Bacca whispered into his ear.

"Oh, yes that's good," Bill said. "Ahem . . . The creepers said you wouldn't *need* the giants anymore, because you golems were going to be so powerful with your cool new items we give you."

The golems continued to leer suspiciously.

"What *kind* of items?" one of them asked.

"All sorts of good stuff," Bill said. "Here, we'll show you."

Bill, Bacca, and everyone else started emptying their inventories. Soon, there was a big pile of all the strange, corrupted items from the Tinkerer's workshop. Bacca gave Bill a thumbs-up. This was going according to plan . . . so far.

"There's all sorts of things here you might like," Bill said to the golems, who had now formed a large half-circle around the pile and were looking on intently. "We've got everything from weapons and armor, to fishing rods, to clocks, to compasses. You can't imagine all the neat things we've got!"

Some of the bolder members of the golem army began picking items up and examining them.

"Yes, go right ahead," said Bill. "There should be more than enough for everybody. Just form an orderly line. No pushing."

The golems began picking through the pile of items like it was an enormous yard sale. Every golem seemed to find something it liked. Some of the golems even took more than one item, which did not bother Bacca in the slightest.

"Er, what do we do now?" Bill whispered to Bacca as the golems began trying out their new toys and trinkets.

"We wait," Bacca said. "And from the looks of it, we won't have to wait very long."

Bacca pointed to a spot in the crowd where two golems appeared on the verge of a fight . . . with each other.

"What did you go and do that for?!" one of the golems said angrily.

"What are you taking about?" barked the other golem sarcastically. "I was just swinging this diamond sword, and for some reason you jumped right in the way of it."

Next, Bacca pointed to another part of the crowd where a different tumult had begun.

"Hey, watch it!" a golem was saying. "You keep snagging my ear with that fishing line."

"That's impossible," said the golem holding the fishing line. "I was casting it in the other direction. It couldn't have hit you."

"Are you calling me a liar?" asked the first golem.

Then a momentous thing happened. The golem with the fishing pole pushed the other golem in the chest. The victim was knocked off his feet and landed on the netherrack floor. He got up and dusted himself off. His mouth curled into a sneer. And his hands curled into fists.

Suddenly, physical disagreements seemed to be erupting all over the island.

"Wow!" said Bill. "This is crazy. They're all fighting with each other."

"Exactly!" Bacca said.

It slowly dawned on Bill that this had always been the plan.

"Okay," Bacca said, calling his group into a huddle. "Here's what we're going to do next. Wizard, I need you to make a bunch more nether blocks— enough for us to craft a bridge back across the lava. Witch, we're going to need all of the same potions we had before. Gargantua and Bill, I need you to keep a look out for any of the golems who might not be distracted, and who might see what I'm about to do."

"What are you about to do?" asked Bill.

Bacca pointed to the top of the hill, where the Dragon Orb hummed and glowed.

"Oh!" Bill said, having momentarily forgotten all about their mission. "Right."

Moments later, Bacca was sneaking through the rows and rows of brawling golems. The corrupted items had quickly caused all kinds of injuries and accompanying insults. Being inherently prideful, Bacca had known that the golems would not let these offenses go unpunished . . . even if the offenders had no idea what they'd done.

Taking full advantage of this confusion, Bacca climbed the hill in the middle of the island and hustled toward the summit. The Dragon Orb was so very near. Then, quite unexpectedly, a grouchy-looking golem stepped out from the other side of the hill.

"Hey," it said. "What are you doing? I'm the only one allowed to be up here by the Dragon O—"

The golem did not have time to finish the sentence. Bacca pulled out Betty with lightning-fast speed, and gave him a surprise chop on the nose. The golem went tumbling end over end down the other side of the hill.

Bacca quickly grabbed the Dragon Orb and stuffed it into his inventory. Then he began running down the hill back to where the rest of his group waited. The majority of the golems continued to fight with one another—they were so thoroughly engaged that they were now no longer sure who had even started the island-wide brawl, or why—but one or two of them noticed Bacca taking the orb, and began calling out to their friends. For the moment their calls were drowned out by the fracas. But Bacca knew that would not last forever.

"I got it," he said as he reached the edge of the lava. "Now we need to get out of here . . . quickly!"

Suddenly a booming voice rang out across the island. It was not quite as loud as Gargantua, but close.

"They've taken the orb!" it cried. "Stop fighting and get them!"

Bacca looked and saw the grouchy-looking golem at the top of the hill. Betty had left a nice big dent in him, but he was apparently still standing. Several of the other golems heard the command. They stopped fighting and began looking around for the culprits.

"All right," Bacca said. "Let's get to it!"

"Here," said the witch, handing out potions. Everyone drank them down and quickly felt much speedier and better able to jump long distances.

A moment later, the lava splashed high in the river. Bacca and the Wizard knew that their window to craft the bridge had just opened. They immediately went to work. A couple of golems—a few of the more clever of the bunch who had realized what was happening before most of their compadres—ran up behind the group.

"Oh no you don't," said the witch, and hit one in the face with potions of harming until it fell to the ground.

"Oh No You Don't," said Gargantua in echo, and lowered his bony foot on one of the sprinting golems, smashing it into a thousand pieces.

"Nicely done," the witch said to Gargantua.

"That Was Fun," the giant agreed.

"Oh no!" shouted Bill.

Everyone turned and saw Bill pointing at a new, much bigger group of golems that had begun to charge. There had to be fifty or more.

"Yikes," said the witch. "I don't have enough potions for all of them."

"And I Have Only Two Feet," Gargantua observed.

Then, much to their relief, they heard Bacca's voice.

"Okay everyone," Bacca said. "Let's go. Just like before!"

Bacca and the Wizard had only been able to build the bridge three quarters of the way across the river of lava. A new lava wave was bubbling up and about to break, and the horde of golems was practically at the foot of the bridge!

Bacca, the Wizard, the witch, Bill, and Gargantua, all leapt off of the edge of the bridge and into the air. Propelled by their potions, they managed to clear the river of lava and land safely on the other side.

Several of the golems followed them out onto the bridge. A few jumped after them. Without potion boosts, they all ended up falling into the river of lava. Most of the rest stood on the partially built bridge, wondering what to do. Then the lava wave came and crashed over them. The golems were set on fire and ran away back onto the island, trying to put themselves out.

Bacca and his group had landed in a heap. For a few moments, they collected themselves, breathing hard. Then there was a sudden realization that spread across them like wildfire. They had done it!

"We did it," said the Wizard. "We got the orb!"

"Yippee," said the witch.

"Yay," said Bill.

"Hooray For Us," said Gargantua.

"Thank you for your help," Bacca said to his team. "I couldn't have done it without you. Well, I mean, maybe I could have. We'll never know for sure. I am Bacca, after all. But thank you for helping!"

The group stood and dusted themselves off. The golems on the other side of the lava were shaking their fists in anger. Bacca and his team prepared to walk back to the Nether Portal and return to the dragons.

"Wait," Bill said. "Now I see what you mean about this place being all right for a hermit. There are lots of nooks and crannies in the walls where people would never think to look for you. And it's so dark and gloomy! Perfect for making people want to stay away. I think I'd like to stay here, if that's all right with you."

"Of course," said Bacca. "I think that's a great idea."

"I Also Will Stay," boomed Gargantua. "In The World Above I Never Saw Giants To Shoot With My Bow. Down Here I Have Seen Several. And Shot Them With My Bow. Maybe There Is More Where They Came From. Plus, Here It Is Always Night. Here, I Like It."

"That sounds fine," Bacca said. "And, of course, if either of you ever change your minds, you can always leave again by exiting through the Nether Portal. Thank you both for all of your help. I wish you the very best of luck!"

Bacca shook hands with Bill, and then shook the end of Gargantua's little finger (which was still a bit too big to properly grip).

"*We're* still coming with you," said the Wizard, as if there were any doubt.

"Oh, absolutely," seconded the witch. "This place is much too dark and smoke-filled for a honeymoon. Ick!"

Leaving Bill and Gargantua to their new home, Bacca, the witch, and the Wizard journeyed back across the Nether until they once again found the portal back to the plane where the dragons dwelled. Bacca leapt through. The witch and Wizard followed. There was a flash as each of them disappeared.

Suddenly, Bacca found himself back atop the highest branch in the forest. The trees all around were covered with dragons. It appeared that all of them had lost the ability to fly. They craned their necks and blinked their eyes, hardly able to believe what they were seeing. Bacca took the glowing Dragon Orb out of his inventory and handed it over to the Diamond Dragon.

"Here you go," said Bacca. "I believe this is yours."

CHAPTER FIFTEEN

Bacca had seen some strange things in his time. But almost nothing prepared him for what happened when the Dragon Orb was once again safe in the claws of the Diamond Dragon.

A glowing light seemed to shoot out from the orb and strike every one of the sickly, exhausted-looking dragons. The moment it touched them, they were magically restored to their former health. Their muscles bulged, their claws gleamed. They took off from the branches and rose high into the sky, making dramatic swoops as they did so. Many of them roared with glee.

"Come on, everyone!" cried the Emerald Dragon. "You know what we have to do!"

The dragons fell into a V formation and flew off into the distance. Only the Diamond Dragon remained.

"Where are *they* off too so quickly?" Bacca asked, scratching his head.

"Let's just say that a few minutes from now . . . the creeper fortress *probably* won't exist anymore," the dragon said with a smile.

The thought made Bacca smile too. Served those mean creepers right. The jerks.

"Anyway, you're welcome," said Bacca.

"Excuse me?" said the Diamond Dragon.

"I was just saying you're welcome . . . for the Dragon Orb that I went and got for you. At great risk and personal expense, I might add."

The dragon looked at Bacca to see if he was being serious. Then it laughed. It was a deep, diamondy sound.

"Oh, our thanks to you are only just beginning," said the Dragon. "But come, first we must return the Dragon Orb to its rightful place."

Bacca hopped aboard the dragon's back, and motioned for the Wizard and the witch to join him. But instead, they remained where they were.

"We think we're going to stay in this forest for a while," the witch said.

"Yes," said the Wizard. "Fresh air. Friendly animals. Nice tall trees. Now *this* is the kind of place where you can have a great honeymoon."

"Oh absolutely," agreed the witch.

"Have a nice time," said Bacca. "Thank you both for all of your help! If you ever need to find me, I'm sure the Diamond Dragon can put you in touch. So long for now!"

With that, the Diamond Dragon rose high into the sky. The Wizard and the witch waved goodbye from the branch below. Bacca held on tight. Empowered by the presence of the Dragon Orb, the Diamond Dragon flew like an arrow through the clear morning sky.

Due to their considerable airspeed, the wind whistling past was quite loud in Bacca's ears. Even so, at one point he could have sworn that in the distance he heard a very great structure being turned into rubble, and hundreds of tiny creeper voices crying out in alarm.

The Diamond Dragon arrived at a beautiful circular palace made of redstone. The dragon landed in a verdant green courtyard in the center of the palace, next to a platform made of blocks of gold. As Bacca looked on, the dragon gingerly placed the Dragon Orb atop the shimmering golden pedestal.

"I don't want to seem bossy . . . but have you thought about a less conspicuous place for it?" Bacca asked. "You don't want it to get stolen all over again, do you?"

"This is the appointed resting place of the orb, where it has sat for centuries," said the Diamond Dragon. "Have no fear. From now on, we will never let it out of our sights."

Just as these words were out of the Diamond Dragon's mouth, Bacca heard the sound of many, many wings approaching. It was all of the other dragons, fresh from their destruction of the creeper fortress. They had very satisfied expressions on their faces.

"The Creep is no more!" announced the Emerald Dragon, alighting near the orb.

"Neither is their fortress," said the Gold Dragon proudly.

"There were some villagers who lived there too, you know," Bacca pointed out. "And sheep."

"Have no fear," said the Emerald Dragon. "We left the innocent unscathed."

"Yeah," added the Lapis Lazuli Dragon. "After all, we're dragons . . . not *monsters*."

"Now we must discuss your reward," said the Emerald Dragon, turning to face Bacca.

Bacca shrugged.

"Actually, if someone could just take me back home now, that would be a great start," Bacca said.

"I miss my friends, and I miss LadyBacc. They'll be wondering where I am."

"But we *must* reward you!" insisted the Gold Dragon.

"You can bring me a reward whenever you like," Bacca said, turning to the Diamond Dragon. "After all, you know where I live!"

"That's true," said the Emerald Dragon.

"Besides, this way it can be a surprise," Bacca said. "It's not as fun when you watch people pick out a present for you. Surprises are much better!"

"Very well," said the Diamond Dragon. "If you are prepared, I can take you back to your home server plane."

"And how!" Bacca said, jumping atop the dragon's back. "Fellas, it's been real. Good luck, and see you later!"

The dragons on the ground waved goodbye as the Diamond Dragon once more soared high into the air. It shot across the landscape, until it found the strange hovering block that would take them back to Bacca's home server. The dragon headed into it. There was a blinding flash, and suddenly they were on the other side. The dragon carried Bacca over a wide blue ocean that was starting to look very familiar. Soon, the towers of Bacca's castle began to rise in the distance.

The dragon landed gently on the highest tower of the castle. The roof was still mostly destroyed from the dragon's first visit. Bacca hopped off the dragon's back and landed back inside his bedroom.

"Thanks for the lift," Bacca said. "Now if you'll excuse me, I feel like I could sleep for ages. I haven't had a chance to fix my roof since your last visit, so let's hope it doesn't rain."

"Sorry again about that," said the Diamond Dragon.

"No worries," Bacca said. "I'm just messing with you. I'll fix it first thing tomorrow morning."

"Very well," said the Diamond Dragon. "I will depart, but you will be seeing me again soon. I don't know if you appreciate just what your actions mean to our community. Your deeds will be remembered for many years to come. For generations, the name of Bacca will ring out from the mouths of dragons, when they recall the greatest, bravest crafter of all time. Young dragons will be taught about you in school. They will . . . they will . . . umm . . . *Bacca*?"

But he was already asleep in his bed, exhausted from his travels, and dreaming about all his adventures and the new friends he had made.

The Diamond Dragon smiled to himself, and flew off into the sunset.

The next day, Bacca was walking through the gardens of his castle with LadyBacc, telling her all about his trip.

"It sounds like those dragons were a lot friendlier than the ones we usually play Dragon Escape with," LadyBacc observed.

"Absolutely," said Bacca. "And they talked more, too."

"I bet you had a really good time," said LadyBacc. "I'm totally jealous. Those dragons must have been so interesting! I wish I could have met one of them."

Suddenly, an unusual shape on the horizon caught Bacca's eye.

"Actually," Bacca said, "it looks like that might be possible."

He pointed skyward. Not one, but *two* dragony-shapes were now making their way across the ocean toward Bacca's castle. By the way the sun reflected blindingly off of its skin, Bacca could tell that one of them was the Diamond Dragon. The other was less reflective, and its body was an unusual orange hue.

And the orange dragon was carrying something in its teeth.

"This is totally awesome!" shouted LadyBacc as the twin dragons circled above.

The dragons slowly descended, eventually landing right next to Bacca in the garden.

"Hello again, Bacca!" said the Diamond Dragon.

"Nice to see you," Bacca said. "Did you notice I've already repaired the 'work' you did to my bedroom roof?"

The Diamond Dragon hung his head.

"I'm just kidding," Bacca said mischievously. "Here, I'd like you to meet my girlfriend. Diamond Dragon, this is LadyBacc."

"I'm pleased to meet you," said the Diamond Dragon, extending his talons in a friendly way.

"Likewise," said LadyBacc, giving them a good shake.

"And I think I know who this might be . . ." Bacca said excitedly, turning to his other guest.

"Yes," said the Diamond Dragon with a smile. "As promised, here is the Pumpkin Dragon."

"Wow!" Bacca said to the Pumpkin Dragon. "I'm so pleased to finally meet you."

"I don't see what all the fuss is about," the Pumpkin Dragon said with a shy smile. "I'm just a dragon made of pumpkins. On our plane, dragons can be made of lots and lots of things."

"I know," said Bacca. "But it's just . . . you're a pumpkin! How cool is that!"

"Oh," said the Pumpkin Dragon. "Well that's a nice self-esteem boost. It actually makes me feel really good about myself, so thanks!"

"We also brought you something," said the Diamond Dragon. With a nod, it indicated a large basket that the Pumpkin Dragon had been carrying in its teeth.

"What is it?" Bacca asked.

"Why don't you open it up and look?" said the Diamond Dragon coyly.

The Pumpkin Dragon took a step back. Bacca carefully opened the top of the basket and an eerie red glow began to emanate from inside. Bacca peeked in, slightly alarmed. Most of the time an eerie red glow wasn't a sign of good things to come. But the Diamond Dragon smiled reassuringly.

"It's okay," said the dragon. "Nothing's going to hurt you."

Summoning his courage, Bacca stuck his hand into the basket and pulled out a series of glowing red ingots. They were unlike anything he had ever seen. He knocked on them with his fist and tested their weight in his hands. They seemed to be stronger than diamonds, and lighter too. It was a totally unknown substance. Confused, Bacca placed them back in the basket and closed the lid.

"What are these?" Bacca asked.

"I don't know if you remember," said the Diamond Dragon. "But when we first met, I told you that if you helped us I would give you an entirely new crafting material. Something you'd never seen before. Something totally unknown to your server plane. Well, here it is. It is a crafting material called Dragonstone."

"Wow . . ." said Bacca, nearly speachless. "Thank you."

"What you decide to craft with it is up to you," said the Diamond Dragon. "But choose wisely. Even in my homeland, Dragonstone is very scarce. Dragonstone weapons and armor are the rarest of all."

"I understand," said Bacca. "I'm honored. Thank you for the gift."

"None of the dragons will ever forget what you did for us," the Diamond Dragon said. "We will always be your friends. You can always call on us if you need anything. Anything at all."

Bacca and LadyBacc looked at each other and smiled. Bacca suspected they had just had the same thought.

"Well," said Bacca. "There *is* one thing you could do . . ."

The Diamond Dragon and the Pumpkin Dragon perched at the edge of the obstacle course that Bacca and LadyBacc had spent the afternoon crafting. The two dragons surveyed the strange expanse, and shared a confused glance. Bacca, LadyBacc, and several of Bacca's other friends stood on a nearby platform. They were looking back at the dragons with great anticipation. Many other people had gathered around the edges of the course, to watch.

"So we just . . . chase you?" the Diamond Dragon asked.

"Exactly," said Bacca. "You come after us, and we have to jump around these obstacles to try and get away. It's really fun. We call it Dragon Escape."

"Yes," added LadyBacc. "It's one of our best games. Usually we play with Ender Dragons from

The End, but you two will be our distinguished guests of honor."

"And we can use our powers of disintegration and destroy the blocks we touch?" asked the Pumpkin Dragon. "These blocks you spent all afternoon building? And you *want* us to do that?"

"Absolutely," Bacca said. "That's the whole point."

"Hmm," said the Diamond Dragon. "If you say so. I guess we're ready."

"Okay, great," said Bacca. "Ready, everyone else? One . . . Two . . . *Three!*"

Bacca and his friends leapt up and started running through the obstacle course. The two dragons took off from their perch and began trying to catch the crafters. Every so often they careened into part of the obstacle course—usually just as a crafter was jumping away from it—and sent the structure exploding into nothingness.

BOOM! Went a row of blocks as the Diamond Dragon smashed through them.

CRASH! Went a platform as the Pumpkin Dragon flew into it and made it disintegrate.

"That's the spirit!" Bacca said as he leapt from platform to platform.

"Yes, I see," the Diamond Dragon cried. "This *is* a very fun game indeed."

Bacca was having the time of his life, and so were his friends. And now even the dragons were apparently enjoying themselves. Everything was like it had been before his adventure . . . But no, that wasn't quite right. Now he had new dragon friends, and friends in another server plane. So maybe, Bacca thought, it wasn't *exactly* like it had been before. Maybe now it was even a little bit better!

Bacca didn't know what he would use the Dragonstone ingots to craft. He realized that that was a big decision. He would think about it carefully for many days before finally selecting something to create. Or maybe he would just leave the ingots in a chest inside his castle, as a souvenir of his trip.

But he definitely knew *one thing* for certain . . .

As he raced across his obstacle course with a big smile across his face, Bacca was confident that the adventures with his new dragon friends were only just beginning!

About the Author

JeromeASF is an Internet personality created by Jerome Aceti, best known for his YouTube Minecraft videos and his character Bacca. Since it was created in 2011, the JeromeASF channel (youtube.com/JeromeASF) has grown to become one of the leading YouTube Minecraft channels around the world, with millions of subscribers and hundreds of millions of views.

DO YOU LIKE FICTION FOR MINECRAFTERS?

Check out other unofficial Minecrafter adventures from Mark Cheverton and Sky Pony Press!

The Gameknight999 Series

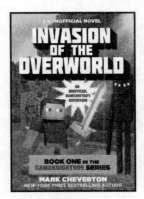

Invasion of the
Overworld

Battle for the
Nether

Confronting the
Dragon

Available wherever books are sold!

DO YOU LIKE FICTION FOR MINECRAFTERS?

Check out other unofficial Minecrafter adventures from Mark Cheverton and Sky Pony Press!

The Mystery of Herobrine Series

Trouble in
Zombie-town

The Jungle
Temple Oracle

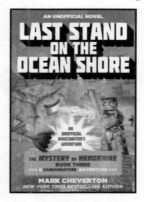

Last Stand on
the Ocean Shore

Available wherever books are sold!

DO YOU LIKE FICTION FOR MINECRAFTERS?

Check out other unofficial Minecrafter adventures from Winter Morgan and Sky Pony Press!

The Unofficial Gamer's Adventure Series

The Quest for the
Diamond Sword

The Mystery of
the Griefer's Mark

The Endermen
Invasion

Available wherever books are sold!

DO YOU LIKE FICTION FOR MINECRAFTERS?

Check out other unofficial Minecrafter adventures from Winter Morgan and Sky Pony Press!

The Unofficial Gamer's Adventure Series

Treasure Hunters
in Trouble

The Skeletons
Strike Back

Clash of the
Creepers

DO YOU LIKE FICTION FOR MINECRAFTERS?

Check out other unofficial Minecrafter adventures from Winter Morgan and Sky Pony Press!

The Unofficial League of Griefers Series

The Secret
Treasure

Hidden in the
Overworld

The Griefer's
Revenge

DO YOU LIKE FICTION FOR MINECRAFTERS?

Check out other unofficial Minecrafter adventures from Winter Morgan and Sky Pony Press!

The Unofficial League of Griefers Series

The Return of the
Rainbow Griefers

The Nether Attack

The Hardcore
War

LIKE OUR BOOKS
FOR MINECRAFTERS?

Then check out other novels
by Sky Pony Press.

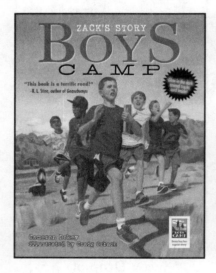

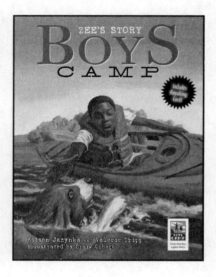

Boys Camp:
Zack's Story
CAMERON DOKEY,
CRAIG ORBACK

Boys Camp:
Zee's Story
KITSON JAZYNKA,
VALERIE TRIPP,
CRAIG ORBACK

Available wherever books are sold!